The Book of Emmaus

Novels by Kevin St. Jarre

Aliens, Drywall, and a Unicycle

Celestine

The Twin

Absence of Grace

The Book of Emmaus

KEVIN ST. JARRE

Encircle Publication
Farmington, Maine, U.S.A.

Paperback ISBN 13: 978-1-64599-349-0
Hardcover ISBN 13: 978-1-64599-350-6
E-book ISBN 13: 978-1-64599-351-3

Library of Congress Control Number (LCCN): 2022933496

Editor: Cynthia Brackett-Vincent

Cover design by Deirdre Wait
Cover photographs © Getty Images

Published by:

Encircle Publications
PO Box 187
Farmington, ME 04938

http://encirclepub.com
info@encirclepub.com

For my mother, Cecile, who always loved history, mysteries, and who often said in response to hearing something new—"Who says?" I love you, Mom.

For my son, Dmitri, who loves history as much as his grandmother did, who is a self-taught expert on some of it, and who was a sounding board for many of the ideas contained in this novel. I hope you like this one, Meetch.

1

MONASTERY OF THE SLAVS
1373

THEY WALKED SIDE by side. Jan Mozara, a fifteen-year-old novice who was not as accustomed to the tunic and scapular as Som Zec was, tried to match the old man's pace. Brother Som had been at the monastery since it was first established, more than twenty-five years before, by the Caesarean and Catholic Majesty Karel IV, the Count of Luxembourg, King of Bohemia, and Holy Roman Emperor.

Jan adjusted his leather belt and tried to center his hood between his shoulders. He was more nervous than uncomfortable.

"Stop pulling at yourself," Som said.

Jan said nothing, and dropped his hands. Som was kind, but easily annoyed. They walked the cloister, the frescoes above them, with parallel scenes from both the Old and New Testaments. In these days since the *pestilencia* came to Prague, the paintings were both comforting and frightening.

The old monk, Som, had been the principle translator at the monastery for many years, and he had been the lead in the effort to translate the Holy Bible from Latin into Czech.

Jan had seen that very manuscript as a child, in this same monastery. How he had stared at it and, even as a boy, recognized the amount of work it represented.

They slowed as they went past the door to the courtyard and entered the Church of Our Lady. They genuflected and made the sign of the cross before they moved into a pew and knelt. Jan knew Som was praying, and that he should be, but instead, he just stared at the floor. When Som once again made the sign of the cross, Jan did as well, and both sat back in the pew.

"Why have we come here at this time of day?" Jan asked.

"Be still," Som said.

The door opened and closed behind them. Jan looked back and saw a monk, not of their order, wearing white. Jan adjusted his own clothing, and Som said again, "Be still." Jan looked forward and waited. The white monk entered the pew behind them.

"Peace be with you," he said softly.

Som nodded. "And also with you."

The white monk asked, "Who is the boy?"

"He is my apprentice," Som said.

"My name is..." Jan said.

Som interrupted, saying, "He does not care."

No one spoke for a time. Jan was not hurt by the rebuke, but the tension and his curiosity were building. Guests from outside the order were rare.

The white monk asked, "Are you prepared?"

"We are," Som said.

"You understand you are not to translate the manuscript. You are only to safeguard it," the white monk said.

"I understand," Som said.

"Knowledge of its presence—or its very existence—is not to be shared even within your order," the white monk said.

"I understand," Som said again.

"Do you understand that, boy?" the white monk asked, tapping on Jan's head. Jan froze, and did not look back.

"Do not touch him," Som said. "He understands."

The white monk said, "Protect the manuscript, but if it becomes necessary, destroy it to prevent it from leaving this place."

"I will," Som said.

"If anyone learns of its existence, deny it. If anyone learns its contents, kill them," the white monk said.

A shudder flashed through Jan's body. How could a brother in Christ speak of murder so, and in a church?

"Surely, it will not come to that," Som said.

"If it does, then you must," the white monk said.

"If it is so dangerous, why not destroy it immediately?" Jan asked.

Som savagely pinched his arm and Jan cried out.

"You mind yourself, or else you will find yourself taking your questions with you," the white monk said.

"Is there anything else?" Som asked.

"Why is this boy even here? I question your judgment already," the white monk said.

"Is there anything else?" Som asked again.

There was a pause, and then the white monk said, "Peace be with you."

"Go in peace," Som said.

The white monk stood and left by the same door through which he had entered.

Jan immediately asked, "Who is he?"

"Whatever you need to know, I will tell you, and only when I feel you need to know," Som said.

"Then, what am I doing here?" Jan asked.

"I am not as young as I used to be. The manuscript may be here longer than I am," Som said.

"I see," Jan said.

"Do not think my bringing you along is some sort of mark of trust or privilege. I chose you because you are young and know little," Som said.

Jan dropped his eyes.

Old Som softened. "Jan, be a sheep for now. You may

need to be a wolf in the years to come, but for now, be silent and watch."

Jan had so many questions, but he held them. Som rose, crossed himself again, and Jan followed him out of the church.

2

EMAUSKLOSTER 1943

THE SKY WAS filled with airplanes. He wasn't really afraid; he was just in awe. The aircraft were likely only being relocated. During the Nazi takeover of Bohemia, more than four years before, Prague had not been bombed. England had traded the Czechs away in exchange for peace with Hitler, and had received none in return. The Luftwaffe could block out the sun above, as German soldiers patrolled Czech streets, and there was nothing anyone could do about it. There was certainly nothing Roman Bily could do about it.

He sat in the garth, the walls rising on all four sides from the edges of the greenery, reaching upwards, framing the twin steeples and a sky alive with German bombers. Still boyish, he looked younger than his years. He planned to live out his life in service to the Lord, if it so pleased God, however long that might be.

Roman rubbed the scar on his neck. Its rough texture and lack of sensation felt like wax stuck on his skin. He looked up at the stonework rising far above him, knowing these walls had been here since the middle of the 14th century. Stability. Permanence. The years living here, with his brethren, had provided the sense of who he was. However, these same walls, which once seemed as if they could hold out the crush of the world, had failed to do so, and more than once. Although the last of the aircraft above passed, and the roar of their engines was fading, Roman knew that directly on the other side of the nearest wall, there were Germans.

He rose and walked slowly across the grass, pushing the green blades this way and that with his toe, examining how they bent. Most of the German men inside came from the Gestapo headquarters, which was a mere twenty-minute walk from the abbey. All Czechs knew that, throughout their history, invaders came and went across their threshold.

As invaders went, the Germans were different. Not especially interested in the land for what it could produce, not here to spread a belief system, and not here for a strategic advantage on a neighboring foe… they seemed to subjugate only for subjugation's sake, and to commit one atrocity after another simply to prove they could. They seemed as interested in psychological conquest as they were in geographical victories.

Roman hoped that they would be soon be gone.

3

EMAUZY 2022

NEVER LOOKING UP from her work, the professor said, “Christophe, this is not Paris. This is Prague. There is a different pace here. Czechs do not rush to wait somewhere. They know there is a certain pace to the world, and one person in a rush cannot accelerate the world around him. You will have to learn to accept it. It might even be good for you.”

Christophe said, “I was at the university a month ago and two visiting professors from New York University were there. They complained that the French were too slow and languid. I suppose the Czechs would be truly frustrating for them.”

Professor Anne Rossignol looked up and smiled. She was a handsome woman, with a streak of grey running through her hair, back to where it was tied. There was an old scar on her right cheek, at which

Christophe was still learning to not stare. She asked, "What did Brother Antonin say about the conference room?"

"He says the earliest we might reserve it is the third Monday of the month," Christophe said. She had asked him to check into renting the conference room for a day, here in the monastery, where the university had already rented them a small office for one year.

The monastery was in Prague 2, on Vyšehradská street, standing through the centuries, known in modern times as Emauzy, although no one seemed to be sure why. The most popular explanation was that long ago, the monks held an annual feast on the day when the Mass included the reading of Jesus's disciples in Emmaus. The exterior walls were a pinkish brown, and had fallen victim, like many walls in Prague, to graffiti. The more conventional steeples had been replaced by two tall sweeping structures, resembling the wings of birds and extending 150 feet into the air. Some people disliked it, some loved it, but it was certainly unique in a city of spires and steeples.

For decades, Emauzy was not a religious place. Under Communism, it had fallen under the control of the Academy of Sciences, but after the collapse of that system all over central Europe, it was returned to its original owners, the Benedictine order. Now, three monks worked in Emauzy, and two of them resided within the walls. It was a small contingent compared to the dozens that once called it home, but at least they were back.

She smiled and said, "That is fine. Please do so. The entire day, please."

"Should I arrange lunch then?" Christophe asked.

"Have lunch catered, yes," she said, and then looked back down at her work. Christophe turned and headed off to find Brother Antonin once more. He felt lucky to be assisting Professor Rossignol in her research; he knew there were many graduate students throughout Europe who had applied to come here and work with her. Before he was notified of his selection, while still in Bordeaux, he knew of at least three other students with him at Université Michel de Montaigne who had submitted requests. To be honest, Christophe was still more than a little surprised that he had been chosen.

4

MONASTERY OF THE SLAVS 1373

JAN LOOKED OUT at the approaching storm with more curiosity than fear. The flashes of lightning in the darkening sky were impressive, and accompanied by great claps of thunder. The wind had shifted and, in the gusts, he could smell the approaching rain. It was less an odor of its own substance, and more the scent of what it had already touched: wet stones, rooves, grass, and less of the usual and disagreeable smells of nature. It was as if the Lord had sent the rain to suppress the vulgar and to lift the pleasant.

There was another flash and, before the thunder sounded, Jan lifted his nose to catch more of the scent. He closed his eyes at the sound, and sniffed at that odd additional smell that only lightning seemed to bring. Perhaps, even though he would never voice such a thought, it was the fragrance of alchemy, the odor of magic.

He opened his eyes at hearing another sound. His brothers were calling out for the door to be opened. Someone was waiting to be let in, just as the rain began to fall. Jan worried when someone was at the door—was it yet another family, carrying a half-dead victim of the pestilencia, desperate for a miracle? He understood that almost all of them were doomed to the same fate, that once the disease entered a home, all inside were likely to fall victim to it. The flock still looked to the church for answers known only to God, but Jan knew the sheep were beginning to doubt.

By the time Jan arrived at the entrance, Som Zec and the other older monks were greeting a man, a fellow Benedictine monk. Soon, the pleasantries having been exchanged, Som and the new arrival stood silent. Without a word, without questions, the other brothers departed, but Jan did not leave. He was nervous and thought he might be sent away, but he remained. He followed when Som and the stranger went into the refectory, and when Jan sat beside Som, the old man patted his thigh.

The stranger's face had been burned long ago, and his left eye had clearly been sewn shut years before. He had a fearsome look, but the softest voice.

"I have brought it," he said.

With his voice marked with concern, Som asked, "Is it in your luggage?"

The stranger glanced with his single eye at Jan, and Jan looked down at the table.

"I have it under my robes, on my person," the stranger said.

Som looked first at one entrance to the refectory, and then at the other. "Give it to me," he said.

"You must guard it with your life," the stranger said.

"I am aware," Som said.

"We fear we are found out. One of my order has already been poisoned, and another, beaten, we believe in an effort to find the text," he said.

Jan crossed himself, and the stranger crossed himself in response, but Som did not.

"I will hide it," Som said. "And tell no one."

The stranger glanced at Jan again.

"He will tell no one," Som said.

The stranger stood, and removed a book from his robes. The cover was leather, but stretched over something rigid, likely wood. It was not very thick. He laid it on the table as one might place an infant. Som did not stand, nor did he touch it. Jan sat and stared.

"If you walk back, past the entrance, and go left down to the end of the hall, you will find the church, so you might pray to our Holy Lady," Som said.

"Why not have the boy show me to my cell?" the stranger said.

Som reached out with one hand, laid it on the book, and said, "Brother Karl, go and ask the Blessed Virgin to watch over you and us, and this, and for your safe return to Regensburg. Then, seek out any of us, and you will be shown where you might sleep."

Karl bowed his head slightly, and left without another word. As he went, Jan whispered, "Peace be with you."

Once Karl was gone, Som slowly stood and slipped the book under his own robes.

"I thought it would be bigger. It is a slight manuscript," Jan said.

"It is big enough," Som said.

"I thought—" Jan said, but stopped.

"What is it?"

"I thought it might be the *Codex Gigas*," Jan whispered.

Som's face twisted, and he asked, "What do you know of the Devil's Bible?"

"Just that a monk, walled up alive, sold his soul to the Devil in order to write it, and that it is very thick, and there is a picture of Satan inside," Jan said.

Som said, "This manuscript is potentially much more dangerous than a copy of the Bible written by yet another mad monk." He patted the cover beneath his tunic.

"But you have not translated it. You have not read it," Jan said. "How can you know it is dangerous?"

"I know because of how afraid Brother Karl is, and by the lengths that so many are willing to go to keep it a secret. Remember, I was instructed to kill anyone who learns of its contents."

Jan shuddered. "Could you?"

Som said, "And I am to destroy it rather than let it escape our walls. Still, such a manuscript has not already been destroyed, which means it must have some truth, some power. There is little that is more dangerous than a thing that you both intensely fear and deeply need, Jan," Som said, and he rose and left.

Pavel, a monk only a few years older than Jan, entered then and sat beside him. Pavel asked, "What is it all about? Who is the stranger? Did old Som tell you?"

While Jan considered Pavel to be his friend, he said only, "The visitor is a messenger, but I have no idea as to the message."

"Secrets," Pavel said. "I have heard rumors of more and more pestilencia in surrounding villages. Perhaps that is the message."

Not wanting to scare Pavel, but having nothing else to offer other than the truth, Jan shrugged and said, "Perhaps."

5

EMAUSKLOSTER 1943

ROMAN SAT WITH Father Cyril Vykoup, the abbot who had come to Emauskloster when it was virtually deserted, and who had grown the community to include two-dozen monks, ten more novitiates, and another thirty lay brothers. He had renewed an interest in the Beuronese liturgy, art, and music. It was the art that Roman and the abbot were discussing, and not the liturgy.

"But why can the artist not be free? Perhaps to experiment? To make the art his own?" Roman asked.

"Such egotism, Roman. The artist must consider the subject, not himself. You know how the artists here collaborate on a single work," the abbot said.

"But then there is no diversion, only replication. What value does that have?" Roman asked.

Before the abbot could answer, the door was thrown

open, and there was suddenly the echoing sound of many boots. Several German soldiers approached, with an officer at the front of the pack, and while Roman stood, the abbot did not.

"Are you Cyril Vykoup?" the officer asked.

"I am," the abbot said.

"I am Hauptsturmführer Friedrich Meinrer of the SS, and have just recently posted here in Prague. I have come in search of something, and I hope you might help us," he said.

"Yes? What is it?" the abbot asked, still sitting.

"You haven't any idea?" Meinrer asked.

"There is precious little gold here," the abbot said.

Meinrer smiled, and said, "We have not come to pry the trinkets from your altar. We are looking for something very old, and more perishable."

"What is it?" Roman asked.

Meinrer looked at Roman briefly, but then at the abbot again, and said, "A book."

The word hung in the air for a moment. No one said a word; no one shifted so much as a foot, except for Roman, who dropped his head.

"We have a small library," the abbot said finally.

"I doubt it would be in there; this is a special book, and very old. It is rumored to have been here for centuries. I find it unlikely that I would know of it, and you, the abbot of this place, would not have even heard of it," Meinrer said.

"What is it called?" the abbot said, but a tremor in his voice gave away that he knew more than he was saying. An expert in lies, the German heard it too, and he smiled.

"If you know where it is, or have any clue to where it might be hidden, I would suggest that you turn that information over to me immediately," Meinrer said.

"Why would someone hide a book?" Roman asked.

Meinrer looked at him again, this time studying him a bit longer, as if he were letting the image of Roman's face be etched more permanently in his memory. Meinrer said, "A book which is said to reveal the true nature of Jesus Christ."

"But is that some sort of secret to be uncovered? He is revealed to all of us every day. The true nature of Christ is known to us, and inside all of us," the abbot said.

"Spare me your mysticism," Meinrer said.

"Why would you want such a book, if it existed?" the abbot asked.

Meinrer paused, and said only, "Call it simple curiosity."

"But your soldiers have been here for years. Why only now do you, personally, come looking for it?" the abbot asked.

Meinrer did not answer, but instead said, "Herr Vykoup, we will begin an exhaustive search of this place tomorrow. We will, of course, try to do as little damage as possible, but we will find this book if it exists. Your cooperation is expected and, if you know where it is, you might save us all a lot of trouble."

"No one here will stand in your way," the abbot said.

There was another pause before Meinrer said, "Yes, I know. I had rather hoped that instead of simply staying out from underfoot, you might be interested in helping us locate what we will undoubtedly find anyway, and then we can be on our way."

The abbot said nothing, and Roman stared at the floor.

After a moment, Meinrer said, "Good day to you both." Meinrer and his men left, slamming the door closed behind them.

"Do you know of such a book? One that reveals Christ to us?" Roman asked.

"Yes, of course," the abbot said.

"And do you know where it is?" Roman asked.

"Of course," the abbot said again. Rising, he walked to a nearby table, picked up a Bible, and said, "Here it is."

Roman nodded, and the abbot smiled and said, "Let's get some water. I am thirsty. We can discuss art a bit more."

6

EMAUZY
2022

CHRISTOPHE KNEW THAT everyone present was an expert translator of historical documents, and he also knew that he didn't have a seat at the table. Professor Rossignol was surrounded by colleagues, each a full professor, from various European universities. They took turns listening, as each one presented what it was he or she was currently working on.

They were seated around a long table at one end of what had once been a refectory. Most of the room was filled with empty wooden seats with red cushions, arranged as if an invisible audience were watching the participants seated around the table.

Christophe, on the other hand, was an assistant. Everyone was very courteous to him—they were polite when they asked him for another few sets of copies of a handout, or for an adapter for a power cord, or inquired whether or not there were peanuts in a particular snack. He felt simultaneously fortunate to be there, and a bit humiliated at his role. Christophe understood that it was likely everyone present had been in his situation before, and that made it easier, but he looked forward to when the excitement he felt every day doing research could be shared with intelligent peers, instead of being treated like an observer who fetches things. Even his chair was set against a wall, and away from the others.

When it was time for Professor Rossignol to share details of her work, she rose and stood in front of the projector screen, although she didn't use it. Instead, she distributed packets of paper. Christophe already had his copy in his lap.

"I am, in fact, searching for an ancient document. I believe that it is hidden within the walls of this monastery," she said. "What you have before you are copies of sources, written throughout the last few centuries, making at least oblique references to the manuscript for which I am searching."

Most flipped through the packets, as if reading them, allowing Professor Rossignol to dramatically pause. "It is perhaps more than a thousand years old, and brought here in the 14th century when the brothers first came to this place."

There were some hushed voices, but no one spoke to Professor Rossignol directly. She continued, and said, "Not to be confused with the Sázava Gospel, now known as the Reims Gospel. It, too, was also originally here, but was spirited away, reportedly to protect it from the Hussites, and made its way to France via Istanbul. This one is different, and perhaps considerably older."

Professor Sabatini asked, "So, you are not translating the document itself? Instead, you are translating these clues in an attempt to find it?"

"That's correct, and I may be on the trail of a translation of the original," Professor Rossignol said.

There was an immediate stirring among the visitors, talking amongst themselves.

"Professor, why don't you let graduate students do that kind of work? And you can work on something more meaningful, less of a… uh… scavenger hunt. You are not even sure if the document you seek exists, or ever existed," Professor Sabatini said.

Professor Tiwari pointed at Christophe and said, "Yes, let him do this kind of work."

Crossing his legs at the knees, Christophe said nothing.

Professor Sabatini asked, "What is the nature of this document? And what are you prepared to do? Go digging about the grounds?"

There were some snickers from around the table, which irritated Christophe. This was not simply some legend; he and the professor had already authenticated and translated many of the documents that referred to the manuscript.

Professor Morris asked, "Is it another gospel, like Reims is?"

Professor Rossignol said, "To be honest—I am not sure." What had been chuckling and murmurs became outright laughter. She said, "But I believe that it is of great enough importance that people have died to keep it secret. I also believe that the Gestapo were searching for this very same manuscript during the occupation."

Professor Tiwari said, "That is hardly supportive of its importance. The Nazis were searching the entire planet for every sort of occult artifact, including the Holy Grail. Unless you are suggesting that perhaps the Grail is here as well?"

There was renewed laughter, and Christophe could not believe how rude they were all being. He was angry, and wanted desperately to come to her defense, but he knew that would only make matters worse. Besides, she hardly needed him to rescue her. Professor Rossignol, for her part, never lost her bearing, and said, "I'm only suggesting that I am on the trail of an historical document, which I believe never left Prague, nor even these grounds."

Every person around the table was talking, and Professor Rossignol looked over at Christophe, who could only shake his head.

Professor Morris raised his hands from the table, and said, "Come now, everyone, a bit of professional courtesy. Thank you, Professor Rossignol. Good luck with your search. Who is next?"

Professor Rossignol returned to her seat, and Professor Tiwari rose to present. The projector came on, and the lights were dimmed.

7

MONASTERY OF THE SLAVS
1373

IN THE COURTYARD, Jan ran his hand across the yellow avens, with the morning dew wet on their petals. Soon, he knew, the sun would rise high enough to dry them.

There was a shout from inside, and then another. Running that way, Jan saw others arriving at the brother's cell, the first few entering but the rest remaining out. As he pushed through to the door, Jan saw Karl in his bed. His face was grey and twisted, and there was vomit on the bedding, with the foulest of odors.

"There is nothing to be done," Som Zec said, turning from the bed.

Many of the brothers around Jan gasped, and all present crossed themselves. Som exited the room, others entered, and they began to pray. As he passed

Jan, Som grabbed the young man's arm and said, "Come with me."

Jan asked, "What killed him? Was it the pestilencia?"

Following Som back out into the courtyard, Jan heard shrieking erupt from where they had just come. They both looked that way, and Som said, "They have discovered the cup."

"Poison?" Jan asked.

"Monkshood," Som said.

Jan crossed himself, and said, "He made a joke of the sin?"

"Perhaps he had come to worry less about sin and, with the manuscript delivered, believed his Earthly work complete," Som said.

"What could make a monk less worried about a mortal sin?" Jan asked.

Som lowered his head, and his voice, and said, "It is a book, written in Glagolitic, that promises to change everything."

"You have read it?" Jan asked.

"Some of it," Som said.

"Is it so awful?" Jan asked.

"If it is the truth, then it is a blessing. If it is a lie, it is certainly a plot more evil than I have ever encountered," Som said.

Saying nothing for a moment, Jan stared at his own feet, until he asked, "What is the book?" He thought Som may snap at him for so many questions, but he did not. In spite of what he had said and the brother's death, Som seemed strangely calm, or at least resolute.

"It is the translation of something very ancient, and I will translate it into Latin. I will keep it hidden," Som said.

"I thought you were instructed not to even read it," Jan said, but then asked, "How long will it take to translate?"

Som said, "It will take as long as it takes." His tone was a bit harsher this time, and Jan understood that he should not press.

Som paused, and then said, "I will keep a journal, notes on my work, and it will include the location of the book. If something were to happen to me, while the others are concerned with prayers and arrangements, find the journal in my cell and keep it safe. Trust and share it with no one. If you cannot promise this, then at least quickly burn my journal, and go on with your service to our Lord."

Jan nodded, and asked, "And what of the book?"

"It will be well hidden," he said. "Swear to protect my journal, or if not, to burn it."

"I swear it," Jan said.

Som nodded, turned, and left.

8

EMAUSKLOSTER 1943

ROMAN AND THE abbot stood in the courtyard, looking at the perennial flowers. The echinacea was still pinkish-purple, but the leucanthemum were long dead.

"The book has not been found, and there are those who believe it no longer exists," the abbot said.

"The Nazis believe it exists," Roman said. "Could it be as simple as it is the Sázava Gospel they are looking for? That they have some source, some reference to that ancient book being here, and they do not realize that they have it already?"

"No, I am afraid they know what they are after," the abbot said.

"It seems Meinrer has come here expressly to find it," Roman said.

"I fear what they may do while looking for it," the

abbot said. He took a sip of his water, and then said, "I do not know where the actual book is, but I do have this." Pulling a small, brown leather diary from his robes, he held it up.

Roman's eyes went wide, the hair stood on his arms, and he asked, "Where did you find it?"

"It does not matter. It is the centuries-old journal of a monk, a translator like you, who lived and worked here for many years. It was encrypted, but someone long ago broke the code, and was led to the book. I checked that hiding place myself, and the book is not there," the abbot said.

"So, you think the journal is of no value?" Roman asked.

The abbot said, "There is more. A follower of Jan Hus had the journal, and perhaps he was last to find, and then hide, the book. I know his name was Vaclav, and he made additional notes in the journal. They, too, are encrypted and I thought perhaps you might be able to make sense of them."

Roman, trying not to seem too eager, asked, "Why not Brother Franta? He has been a translator here since long before I arrived."

"He is a talented linguist, but you have shown more of a gift when it comes to breaking encryption, you've always shown a keen interest in the history of this place, and when you read this and see the nature of the missing book, you might understand. I fear Franta's faith is not as… elastic as yours, and he is old. I would hate to sow seeds of doubt in one who may not have the time to overcome them," the abbot said.

"I see," Roman said.

"You must swear on your soul to protect the journal, with your life if need be," the abbot said.

Roman closed his eyes, as if pained, and then said, "I swear it."

Hesitantly, the abbot handed the journal to Roman, and said, "Hide it beneath your robes, take it to your cell, and report to me tomorrow your progress with Vaclav's notes. Do not waste time with the entire journal; I have already read it. Frankly, I considered tearing Vaclav's notes from it to give to you, but I thought it better to keep them together."

Roman stared at the cover, and rubbed the leather. He seemed lost in thought for a moment, as if it reminded him of something.

"Hide it," the abbot said.

Roman slipped the journal beneath his robes, and said, "I will do my best."

"Go to your cell and get started. We must find the book before the Germans do," the abbot said.

9

EMAUZY
2022

"THEY WERE INCREDIBLY impolite. I thought it was very unprofessional of them," Christophe said.

"They like to think that professors are above certain work," Professor Rossignol said, smiling. "After all, that's why we have interns."

Knowing she didn't really feel that way, he asked, "It doesn't bother you?"

"My self-esteem is not built upon the opinion and comments of people like Anil Tiwari," she said.

"When we find the book, they will claim that they never doubted you," Christophe said.

"And I certainly don't want to find it in order to impress them," she said.

"If what we have learned turns out to be true, I think everyone will be interested," he said.

"If we find it, and if it is intact, that may be true. I wish I knew what it contained, but the sources seem to speculate that it may shake the faith of some people," she said.

There was a pause, and then Christophe asked, "Do you ever wonder if perhaps it should not be found? The immediate ramifications for two billion Christians may be overwhelming, and there would be a ripple effect into the non-Christian world. I mean, nearly one third of the Earth's human population claims to believe that Jesus was the Christ."

"I doubt the impact would be *that* profound. It may change some facets of what they believe, and perhaps impact somc of the more exaggerated stories, but I do not believe that any document could cause devout Christians to abandon their churches," she said. "Besides, it is not up to us to protect people's faith. We are simply searching for an historical document, and I might add we are guessing as to its scope. All we have are vague hints as to its content."

After another pause, Christophe said, "Ah, we are not really closer to finding it anyway. The work we have done and the documents we have translated have added support to the existence of the manuscript, but there have not been any clues as to its current location."

Professor Rossignol sat beside him, took a deep breath, and said, "I will be meeting with someone tomorrow who claims to have pages from a journal which may lead us to it."

"Who?"

"I cannot say," she said.

"Why doesn't he retrieve the manuscript himself?" Christophe asked.

"He says if it is to be revealed to the world, that he does not want to be the one to do it. He does not want this spotlight on him," she said. "It could also be that he has tried already and failed."

"Are we sure we want to be the ones in the spotlight?" Christophe asked.

She laughed, and said, "You are right. I will turn down his offer and not meet with him."

Christophe froze, laughed, and said, "No, of course, but is it safe to meet with a stranger? How did he even know what you are looking for? You just yesterday revealed it to the others. Perhaps I should come with you."

"He said he would meet with me alone," she said.

"All the more reason not to," he said. "Tell me who it is."

"I cannot tell you," she said. "I will meet him at noon tomorrow, and I will come straight here afterwards."

"I really wish you'd let me come along," Christophe said.

Professor Rossignol smiled and said, "It will be alright."

10

MONASTERY OF THE SLAVS 1373

THIS TIME, IT was not merely a family, or even a crowd, but instead a mob outside the monastery. So many voices, it was difficult to understand their shouting, but their feelings were clear. They were enraged because the church had not been able to protect them from, nor find answers regarding, the pestilencia.

"They will not be sent away, neither with words of comfort nor calls for prayer," Som said. "They will not leave, until they have taken something from this place."

"What should we do? Should we pray?" Jan asked.

Som said nothing for a moment, but then smiled, patted Jan on the arm, and said, "Of course." Reaching then into his robes, he produced a small book. It was not the larger manuscript the monk had delivered; the leather cover was as pliant as the pages within. Som handed it to Jan.

"Why are you giving this to me? Is this your record of the translation?" Jan asked.

"Keep the journal safe," Som said.

"Where are you going?" Jan asked.

"I hope that you will be able to return it to me shortly," Som said.

The shouting grew louder, and the sound of human hands beating on the door was replaced with the pounding of stones or tools. Som went that way, and Jan began to follow him. Som turned and said, "No, Jan, go and pray, as you said."

Jan saw Pavel approaching, and hid the journal under his tunic. Som made his way to the entrance.

"What will he do?" Pavel asked.

"I am not sure," Jan replied.

Just as Som got there, the door burst open and the mob rushed in. Som raised his hands as they encircled him, and one of the men closest to Som struck him in the head with a rock the size of a fist. He went down, disappearing beneath them.

Jan took a step toward Som and his attackers, but Pavel grabbed Jan from behind. The other monks were shouting and scattering in all directions, as the mob looked for others upon whom to vent their fear and rage.

"Let me go!" Jan said.

"There is nothing to do! We must hide! They will kill us all!" Pavel said.

Jan struggled, but then as the people began to run at him and Pavel, they both fled. Down the corridor, past the chapel, and quickly into the narrow slit of a passageway that led to a small, windowless chamber. The monastery had a few of these hidden passageways, barely wider than the depth of a man's chest. In fact, many of the better-fed monks could no longer pass through them. The mob went by, unaware of where the young monks had turned.

"Is there any chance Som is still alive?" Jan asked, still catching his breath.

Pavel did not answer. In the distance, somewhere within the walls, a man cried out in short-lived agony.

They stayed hidden there, into the night, as the monastery around them grew terribly quiet.

"How can they just kill like that, and men of God?" Jan asked. "Som never hurt anyone. He was likely going to try to bring peace and comfort to them, and they…killed him."

"They are afraid. For most, fear will turn to anger after a time, and with the courage of a mob, they brought their fear-madness here," Pavel said.

Jan was silent a moment, wiped a tear, and then said, "When I was younger, before I came to this place, my brother Petr and I were in the village, and there was a crowd, but not at the market. In the square, they had erected gallows to hang a man. He was an old cobbler, his hands were bound together, and he yet protested his innocence, but it was decided. The man in charge, whom I had never seen before, said that the cobbler had been condemned on the sworn testimony of a wealthy man, an important merchant, who we knew to come to our village only seasonally. But his testimony was enough."

Pavel said, "It has always been that way."

"But words are words. There was no evidence, and yet one man's words were enough to hang another, and the cobbler's words were not enough to save him," Jan said.

"Old Som's words could not save him either, and he had words in so many languages. Within these walls, with his brothers, his words had carried such weight, but when that frenzied mob entered, they never gave his protestations a moment's pause before striking him down. Maybe they had to hurry to attack him before his words could have any effect. Perhaps they sensed that his words might soothe their anger, their madness, and leave them only with the pure fear it had earlier been," Pavel said.

"You believe they struck him dumb and dead to protect their rage?" Jan asked, his voice cracked, and tears fell.

Pavel said, "Perhaps."

Jan said, "It is remarkable that their fear of the

pestilencia is greater than their fear of mortal sin."

"In their minds, which is the closer threat?" Pavel asked.

Jan did not answer for a moment, and then said, "They may tally up, the plague and the sin, on the same night."

11

EMAUSKLOSTER 1943

THE GERMANS WERE a constant presence, at first searching through books for a false cover, next going through every cupboard and closet, and then they had begun to tear into the walls of every space that showed signs of having been bricked or plastered over since the original construction.

Roman had overheard the soldiers talking, saying that they were beginning to doubt the book would ever be found. Others complained that the abbot and the brothers must know where the book was, and that they were likely hiding it.

No monk resisted Meinrer and his men, but nor did they help in any way. The tension during each day of searching was worse than the last, until it boiled over. On that day, the soldiers came in, and collected everyone in the Church of Our Lady. The brothers stood huddled together, the abbot in the front, with Roman a bit behind him, facing the Germans whose weapons were leveled at them. Meinrer himself, off to one side, said, "Disrobe."

There was whispering and murmuring among them, but no one did anything. Meinrer said, "I said to disrobe. Leave all of your clothing at your feet, and move to the altar."

The abbot was first to act, and he began to take off his clothes. The others followed his lead. Roman was terrified for them all, and as he undressed, he looked from statues to paintings within the church as if help might come.

The naked men moved closer to the altar, self-consciously covering their genitals with their hands. A few of the German soldiers moved forward and quickly searched all of the clothing for any sign of the book. Roman had left the journal in his cell, hidden in plain sight among a few books the Germans had already searched through.

Once the clothes had been searched, the Germans left them on the floor. His voice flat, Meinrer said, "Get dressed." Roman thought the Germans would leave the church at that point, but instead they watched the monks put their robes back on.

"My dear abbot, I have decided that you and your monks are needed elsewhere. We will remain, and continue our search, and the Deutsches Rotes Kreuz will set up a hospital here in your monastery," Meinrer said.

"But where will we go?" the abbot asked.

"You can continue your ministry among a different flock, where you will join a great many members of the clergy, from around the Reich. You will be taken by train to Bavaria, to a camp outside Munich, called Dachau. You will not be permitted to return to your chambers; you will be leaving directly from here," Meinrer said.

"You cannot do this," the abbot said.

"Perhaps if you and your monks had been a bit more useful, I would have seen a reason to keep you here, but at best you have been underfoot, and at worst you have secretly worked against our effort," Meinrer said.

The brothers were talking among themselves, loudly and upset, but none had taken a step. Roman gripped a bit of the abbot's robes. Meinrer nodded to his men, and they began to take the monks away, but then Meinrer grabbed Roman's elbow.

"You will stay," Meinrer said.

The abbot turned, his facial expression heavy with concern as he and Roman locked eyes for a moment, and then a soldier shoved the abbot to keep him moving. Roman watched as the brothers were driven out, and then found himself alone in a silent church with Meinrer and one other soldier.

"You will stay on as a caretaker, and as my house

boy," Meinrer said. "I will move my quarters here, and I need someone who knows this place."

Roman said nothing; on top of the fear for the monks and the abbot, and anger, he now felt guilt at being allowed to remain.

"You will be expected to work," Meinrer said, but then added, "Someday, you may even come to feel gratitude."

Meinrer stared at Roman for a moment, said nothing, and then the officer walked out of the church. Roman looked back at the altar, walked over to it, and knelt in prayer.

12

EMAUZY
2022

THE NEXT DAY, mid-afternoon, Professor Rossignol came to the office carrying a yellow envelope. Christophe could barely contain himself, and asked, “What did you learn?” She went to her desk, and Christophe followed. From the envelope she pulled hand-written pages.

“These are pages from the journal. See the notes on the pages and in the margins? The original journal dates from the 1370s, and was itself written in a code, which has been broken, and these additional encrypted notes were written supposedly by a Hussite named Vaclav, who worked to decipher the journal in order to find the book,” she said.

“There appears to be a few other marks in the margins,” Christophe said.

“Someone between the 15th century and today also

had a look, maybe an attempt to break the Hussite's code, but didn't write the solution for us. The marks that person made were only for himself," she said.

"Maybe it was the source who gave you these pages," Christophe said.

"I suspect the newest notes are a few decades old," she said.

Christophe said, "And you can't tell me who gave you this?"

She didn't answer, but then said, "Let's start by making copies of these pages, and then we can begin to work on it ourselves. I suspect the original text will reveal the history, while the Hussite's notes might lead us to the book's current location."

"If no one has moved the book in the subsequent 600 years?" Christophe asked.

"You are ruling out that someone may have moved it, and then returned it to the same hiding place," she said.

"Why would they do that?" he asked.

Professor Rossignol smiled, and said, "So that we might find it."

13

MONASTERY OF THE SLAVS
1373

BY MORNING, THE madness that had brought the mob inside the walls was gone and, just as with drink, nothing remained but silence and guilt. The people left the fallen monks where they lay, the living ones where they were hidden, and retreated to their homes. Mercifully, there had been only one small fire that did little damage save for the smoke, and it smoldered in one corner of the refectory.

The brothers came out of hiding, and began praying and crying over those who had been lost. Jan and Pavel ran to the side of Som Zec, who lay with an ugly injury to his head, and footprints all over his body.

Holding Som's sleeve, Jan cried while Pavel prayed. Wiping his tears on Som's cold hand, Jan said, "What can we do now?"

"We will give them all a proper burial," Pavel said, "Then, we will have to decide if we will leave this place."

Remembering Som's journal, and the book, Jan knew he could not leave. "I will stay," he said.

"The people may return, and murder us out of guilt and self-hatred. Having sinned already, it will be easier for them," Pavel said.

"I have to stay," Jan said.

Pavel said nothing for a moment, and then asked, "What is it that will keep you here?"

Jan examined Pavel's face for a moment, and then said, "I have a secret to share with you, but first we must bury poor Som."

The two young men carried the old monk's body to the graveyard, and there they buried him. Before Som disappeared into the earth, Jan kissed his forehead. Pavel said nothing. Others buried three more brothers nearby. The soil smelled fusty, but the air was cool and fresh. They prayed together over each grave. Unlike Jan, most of the others had resolved to leave. They spoke of destinations, of family and other monasteries, but most seemed dazed, and of having false confidence. Between disease and all the other hazards of the outside world, nothing was certain. It was unlikely that they would ever see each other again, especially the older monks, so there was much embracing and kissing.

After most had left, except for the oldest among

them who were resigned to stay, Jan followed Pavel to the courtyard. Once there, in one corner, he turned and asked, "What is the secret?"

He seemed too eager, and it unnerved Jan. Before they buried Som, Jan had intended to show Pavel the journal, but now Jan was unsure and said, "There is a secret hidden here in these walls."

"What is it?" Pavel asked.

Jan hesitated, and Pavel said, "If you do not want to, then do not tell me." He was clearly frustrated.

Although Jan was still uncertain, he slowly removed the journal from his robe, and showed Pavel.

"Is this the secret?" he asked, reaching for it.

"This is Som's journal. Inside are his notes. He was translating something—a book he has hidden in this place," Jan said.

Pavel flipped through it, and said, "It is written in some sort of code."

"Yes," Jan said.

"Can you decipher it?" Pavel asked.

"We will work on it," Jan said.

"How long will it take?" Pavel asked.

"I am not certain. Som meant for me to have this if something happened to him, so he must have had confidence that I could break his code," Jan said, and slipped the journal back into his robe.

14

EMAUSKLOSTER
1943

IT WAS NOT the same without the abbot and the brothers. Had he been isolated, that would've been one thing; Roman had lived a solitary life before. However, the grounds were teeming with people. He was not alone, and the only language spoken was German. The walls had long echoed with Czech and Latin, and many other European languages. Roman remembered the young Swedish monk, an artist and scholar, who had added white stripes with text to the frescoes in the hallways; they were captions of a sort, explaining the scenes depicted in each.

But, with the absence of his brothers, only the language of the occupiers remained. It was not the first time the German language had dominated Czech within the monastery, but it was the first time the language was absolutely uncontested. Even Roman was forced to speak it and, to him, it tasted like moldy bread in his mouth.

He walked into the Church of our Lady, and frowned at the transformation. The pews had been adapted into hospital cots, but here at least were not the soldiers in their uniforms of grey or black. These were women, members of the DRK, or German Red Cross; they were nurses preparing for casualties. The women spoke softly, as if in reverence to where they knew they were, but there were still all the noises of unpacking and arranging. Wooden crates were pried open, steel trays were stacked, and glass bottles clinked.

Roman put his hand on a stone pillar; the cool, rough surface was solid, and promised that, just as it had weathered six centuries of tumult, it would stand through this.

"Have you ever heard any of the monks, or the abbot, speak of secret doors or passageways? Perhaps a hidden cellar?" a voice behind him said. Roman turned, and Meinrer was standing a few feet away.

"I have heard stories, but just stories," Roman said, guessing that Meinrer might have heard one as well.

"And you have no idea where these stories might have suggested passages might be?" he asked.

"Never. I think they are just stories," Roman said.

"Still, I know you are hiding something," Meinrer said. "My patience is at an end. If I have to, I will dismantle this building, stone by stone."

"Sir, I honestly do not know of any secret doors," Roman said.

Meinrer stared for a moment, looked out at the nurses, and left. When Roman turned, all of the nurses had stopped working and were staring at him. Even they looked frightened. Roman walked among them and said, "I have not been ordained, but if you would like, tomorrow morning, Sunday, we could pray together in this place. It is the Church of Our Lady."

Most of the nurses returned to their work without saying anything, but then one stepped out from behind another pillar, and said, "I would pray on Sunday with you." She was beautiful, with her brown hair coming together under a white cap. The bluish grey dress, beneath a white apron, closed at her delicate throat with a brooch bearing a red cross. Her skin was creamy, her lips full, and her eyes were a golden-green.

"How are you called?" Roman asked.

"Renate Müller," she said.

"Very well. Tomorrow," he said.

"Should I call you Brother, then?"

"Please," he said.

Her brow furrowed. "What is your name?"

He hesitated, and then said, "Roman Bily, but again, please…"

"Brother Roman, fine," she said.

"Thank you. In the morning," Roman said, "Bring friends if you like."

A nurse behind her chuckled, and Renate said, "I'm afraid I haven't any."

Roman looked at the other nurses, and then back at Renate, and said, "Neither have I. I'll see you tomorrow morning."

* * *

The next morning, Roman met Renate near the altar.

"It doesn't feel like a church anymore," she said.

There were white sheets everywhere, and the smell of disinfectant hung in the air. Roman said, "We can move into the Imperial Chapel." He led her through a door, into a tiny anteroom, and then into a small chapel with only a few rows of pews. The only windows were on their left. Behind a modest altar covered with a white cloth was a tall archway, and painted within it was a depiction of the crucifixion. Christ was on the cross, surrounded by his mother, Mary Magdalene, and other followers.

"A deer," Renate said.

"A deer?"

"Behind the cross… instead of a lamb, there is a deer," she said, pointing.

Roman looked, "Ah yes, I thought that an odd choice."

"I agree. Jesus was like the lamb; he was passive even in death. A deer would not be, but instead would flee," she said.

Roman stood staring, until Renate said, "Should we pray, Brother?"

He looked at the deer a moment more, and then they knelt together in a pew. He asked, "Should we pray in German?"

"I will not say anything. Pray for us both," she said.

In German, Roman recited this prayer,

"Soul of Christ, sanctify me.

Body of Christ, save me.

Blood of Christ, inebriate me.

Water from the side of Christ, wash me.

Passion of Christ, strengthen me.

O Good Jesus, hear me.

Within Thy wounds hidc mc.

Suffer me not to be separated from Thee.

From the malignant enemy, defend me…"

Renate looked up at this, but then closed her eyes, and lowered her head once more. Roman continued,

"In the hour of my death, call me.

And bid me come unto Thee,

That with all Thy saints,

I may praise Thee forever and ever.

Amen."

"Amen," she said, "I haven't heard that prayer before."

"I learned it a long time ago," Roman said.

"Could you hear my confession?" she asked.

"You do not need me, or even a priest, to confess

before God and have absolution. You can confess in the privacy of your own chamber and, if you are contrite and honest, the Lord will forgive you," Roman said.

Renate sat in the pew and said, "That's a strange thing to say. I thought the sacrament required a priest."

"So say the priests," Roman said. "If God loves us so much, why would he want separation from us? Why have an intermediary?"

Renate laughed at this, and Roman smiled. "You're a very strange monk," she said.

"I've been told that before," he said.

She was quiet a moment, and then asked, "Why do you think Meinrer chose you to stay behind? It would have perhaps made more sense to keep the abbot."

"Maybe he thought that I would be more likely to reveal secrets than the abbot would," Roman said.

"You do not seem the type to give up secrets," she said.

"You hardly know me," Roman said.

"I can tell."

Roman paused, and then asked, "Why have you come here? Did you choose to come to Prague?"

She looked at the floor, and said, "I lived not far from here. In Germany, near a city called Ansbach, a place called Katterbach. My husband and I took over his parents' farm, and his mother lived with us. There was an airfield next to the farm. I remember watching my husband stand out in the field, watching the planes take off and land. He would be transfixed, sometimes not taking a step for an hour, not working, just watching."

"He became a pilot," Roman said.

Renate nodded, and said, "Yes, a year after we were married."

Both sat silently for a moment, and Roman said, "You don't need to tell me any more."

"How he loved to fly," Renate said, looking up, and then she smiled. Wiping her tears, she said, "After… I lost him… his mother went to live with her brother in Augsburg, and I joined DRK."

"How did you become a nurse?" Roman asked.

"By nursing," she said. "I have never been to university, so I suppose I am not a proper nurse, but I do what I can. Many of the other women are the same."

"Why don't you have friends among them?" Roman asked.

"I suppose some are friendly, but many distrust me because I refuse to join the party. I am not supportive enough, they say. I am not a political person; I only wanted to live my life as a farmer's wife. Now, the only cause I have is to provide comfort to those I can, and to pray this all ends soon," she said.

There was another moment of silence, and then she asked, "How did you come to be here?"

Roman said, "I came, in the first, because I have

always had facility with language, and my father knew that the Benedictine order here was doing important work. My oldest brother was in line to take over the family's holdings, and the next went into military service. So, I came to serve God."

"Is your brother still a soldier?" Renate asked.

"No, he was lost some time ago," Roman said.

"Oh, I'm so sorry. Here I am talking about my husband, and you have suffered as well, and likely at the hands of my countrymen," Renate said.

"Please. It was not in this war," Roman said.

Renate cocked her head, apparently considering this for a moment, and then he said, "Should we pray some more?"

"If you would like," she said, and both went to their knees once again. Roman prayed, both in German and in Latin, while Renate bowed her head, hands clasped together. After some time, Roman stopped, and looked at Renate, who smiled. Roman nodded, and smiled in return.

"This was nice. Thank you, Brother Roman," Renate said.

"You are welcome," Roman said. "Perhaps we can do it again."

She took his hand in hers, and said, "I'd like that."

There was a bit of an awkward pause, and then they both exited the pew, genuflected, and left the chapel.

"Good day," Roman said.

"See you later," she said.

They parted, and Roman slowly walked down the corridor toward the refectory, contemplating. He wondered where the book was. The original notes in the journal said that it was hidden beneath a stone at the base of the refectory window farthest from the entrance, but he knew it was no longer there. Before entering the room, Roman looked both ways, and saw no one. Stepping inside, he moved slowly and seemingly without purpose. Down the center of the ceiling, a line of electric light fixtures hung like modest chandeliers. The refectory, once filled with the aroma of fresh bread and the sounds of men eating, was completely silcnt and smelled only of want.

The large windows were across the room from the entrance, and were only beginning to light as the sun shifted from the eastern horizon into the southern sky. Roman moved to the farthest and looked at the sill. It was modern. Still stone, it was a single thin industrially cut piece, matching the other windowsills exactly. Although the windows had not been replaced, the original windowsill stones were gone, and so was the book. Roman looked up at the leaded glass, and thought that if the Hussite's notes did not reveal where the book was, it may be lost forever.

Roman returned to his cell. It was cool, and smelled of linen. Pulling three books from the stack on his bedside table, he lay on the bed. He was not interested in two of them, but opened them anyway, and laid them on the bed. The third was the journal. The familiar original writing, with the decoded notes above, was there; he'd read those many times, but Roman turned to the notes left by Vaclav the Hussite.

Vaclav had used, in 1424, a polyalphabetic cipher. Roman knew that most historians would claim this was decades too early, but he had personally seen and worked on polyalphabetic cyphers dating back to the 12th century, especially in Arabic texts.

Roman also knew that it meant it would take longer to solve the encryption. A monoalphabetic cypher would have meant that each letter in the alphabet had a fixed and constant substitute. Every child had played with these; they shifted every letter by one place in the alphabet so that A became B, B became C, and so on. A simple polyalphabetic cypher could mean that there was key progression, meaning it might change with each letter. For the first letter, the key might list A as B, and for the second letter, the key would change and A would become C, for example. In a message using 300 words, comprised of 1,200 letters, there might be 1,200 key changes.

Roman began working on it, pausing each time someone walked by the door to his cell. The soldiers' boots were so much easier to hear than had been the sound of monks walking. He had begun to make some progress when there was a knock at the door, and then someone attempted to open it. The knock immediately became a pounding. Roman slipped the journal into the stack on the bedside table, leaving the two open books on his bed. When he opened the door, it was Meinrer.

"Why was this door locked? You know this is forbidden," he said.

"Sorry. It's force of habit," Roman said.

"Break the habit."

"Yes, I will try," Roman said.

There was a moment's pause, and then Meinrer said, "We have decided the book we seek is likely in the refectory. We will begin digging up the floor tomorrow. You can prevent this if you can tell me where the book is," Meinrer said.

The refectory? Roman had gone there right after praying with Renate. Had she followed him? Had someone else? The coincidence was too great.

"I have no idea where the book is," Roman said.

Meinrer said, "Very well."

Roman said nothing.

"Leave this door open. Understand?"

Roman nodded, but Meinrer was already walking away.

15

EMAUZY
2022

WHEN THE KNOCK came on the office door, Christophe had no idea who it was.

"Let him in," Professor Rossignol said.

When Christophe opened the door, a man in a suit entered, and said, "Good morning."

"Good morning," Professor Rossignol said, standing.

"I am Lieutenant Hynek Potok, with the Criminal Police and Investigation Service. Are you Professor Anne Rossignol?" he asked.

"I am, and this is my assistant, Christophe Thibodeau," she said.

"I understand you have received a threat," Potok said.

"Please sit," Professor Rossignol said, and they all did.

"What threat?" Christophe asked.

She pulled a letter from her desk, and offered it to

Potok, "I received this yesterday. It's obviously not signed."

He did not take it, but instead pulled a plastic bag from his pocket and let the professor drop the letter inside. "Has anyone but you touched it?" he asked.

"Only me," she said. "And I assume the postman, and everyone else between the sender and me."

Potok froze, and studied the professor's face for a moment. He then asked, while sealing the bag, "Do you have any idea why anyone would threaten you both?"

"Both?" Christophe asked.

"The letter, as you'll see, suggests we should give up the search for a certain book that we suspect is hidden here in the monastery," she said.

"It threatened both of us?" Christophe asked again.

Potok glanced at him, but then turned back to Professor Rossignol and asked, "Who might want you to stop searching?"

"We aren't sure what the book is yet, but there are not many people who know the nature of our work," she said.

"The people at the day conference?" Christophe asked.

"Conference?" Potok asked.

"We held a one-day meeting to discuss the work of those professors who attended. I presented our work as well, and discussed the search for the book," she said.

Potok asked, "What was the reception from the rest of the group?"

"Hostility," Christophe said. Professor Rossignol looked at him in a way that conveyed that she'd like to be the one to answer the questions.

"From all of them?" Potok said, taking out a notepad.

"No, perhaps only from two," she said.

"What are their names?" Potok asked.

"I'd rather not get into all that. I'm sure they wouldn't threaten physical harm. They mocked the search, but didn't ask us to stop," she said.

"Actually, they did suggest you, yourself, stop, and turn it over to a student," Christophe said.

"Please. The names of the two colleagues," Potok said.

"Drs. Anil Tiwari and Ottavio Sabatini," Christophe said, and Professor Rossignol sighed.

"Do you have contact information for them?" Potok asked. Professor Rossignol looked in a drawer and withdrew a few business cards, before handing two of them over to Potok.

"Thank you," he said, "But you don't believe that they could be responsible?"

"I can't imagine anything like this from anyone who was there," she said.

"And have you made any progress in finding the book?" Potok asked.

"Some, but nothing definitive yet," she said.

Christophe wondered if she would mention the journal pages, and the person who had supplied them, but she didn't.

Potok stood and said, "Thank you for your time. If I have any additional questions, I will call. If you receive another note, please handle it as little as possible, and call us right away. Also, if you think of anyone else who might want you to abandon your work, please let us know."

"I will," she said.

"Thank you," Potok said, and left.

Christophe turned to her, and asked, "What, exactly, did the note say?"

She said, "It read that we should give up the search for the book. That if it exists, if it is what some say it may be, it could undermine the church."

"Which church?" Christophe asked.

"I assume the Roman church," she said.

"Still, it's not a threat to us. It's only a warning that..."

"It went on. The author said that the protection of the faith was more important than the careers, or even lives, of two academics," she said.

Christophe eyes widened. "It said that?"

"So, I spoke to the chair at the university, and she told me to call the local police. I have done so, and now we can return to our work," she said.

"But the police are not providing any protection?" Christophe asked.

"What would you have them do? Post guards?" she asked, and he immediately felt foolish. "Let's get to work on the journal," she said.

16

MONASTERY OF THE SLAVS 1373

JAN AND PAVEL were in Jan's cell, with the journal lying open on the rough little table. Pavel stood against one wall, while Jan stared intently at the pages.

"This might be an 'L'," Jan said.

Pavel sighed, and said, "Congratulations. Two days of work, and you may have deciphered a twelfth letter," he said.

"With each new letter, deciphering the next becomes easier," Jan said.

"Why did the old man conceal his notes, anyway?" Pavel asked.

"He did not want just anyone to find the book. In fact, he was instructed to destroy the book before letting it fall into the hands of others. I heard this myself. Also, Som was to protect the book with his life," Jan said.

"Well, he has done a fine job of hiding it," Pavel said. "What use is a book that no one should be allowed to see?"

Jan sat back, and was quiet for a moment.

"What is it?" Pavel asked.

"I wonder if we should see it," Jan said.

"We have to see it, so that we might judge whether or not to destroy it, or to leave it hidden," Pavel said.

"Who are we to judge that?" Jan asked.

Pavel said nothing, and then Jan said, "Perhaps it would be best if we stopped, and if we burn Som's journal. I am not sure that Som would want us to continue."

Pavel stepped forward, and said, "We cannot stop."

"Why not?"

"Because someday, even if only by chance, the book will be found," Pavel said. "And it could be found by anyone. What if someone who meant to harm the Church found it? Or what if there are wonderful secrets in it, perhaps even a cure for the pestilencia?"

"Why would Som hide such a blessing?"

"Because he swore to. Because he was old, and would see even the illness as the will of God," Pavel said.

"Don't you see it that way?" Jan asked.

"I see it as the work of the devil," Pavel said. "Maybe the book is God's deliverance from the pestilencia, and these old fools have hidden it from us. Maybe the disease is from the devil, and the book is from God."

Jan said nothing, and picked up the journal.

"We have to find it," Pavel said. "We will find it, read it, and then decide what to do with it, acting as God's humble servants. We will pray for his guidance in all things."

"Humble, yes, and sober. We must fight the urge to act on what our hearts are telling us, and to rely on our minds, and on our faith. Even if there is a cure to the pestilencia in the pages, even that would be a powerful thing," Jan said.

"Think of the death and misery that would prevent!" Pavel said.

"True, but think if even a single person, a despot, had that information and could control who gets the cure and who does not. It would give him enormous power over everyone—over kings, and even over the Holy Father. It would literally be the power to kill or save masses of people, across borders, across the seas, from here to the Holy Land, at his choosing. We must be measured and cautious, Pavel," Jan said.

"We will be," Pavel said.

"The reverse is also true. There are evil men, even now, who use fear of the sickness to control their people. Knowledge of a cure would undo that power. Those evil men would surely attempt to put doubt into the minds of their followers about a cure, perhaps to portray the cure as evil, and this could pit brother against brother, cousin against cousin, region against region. There is much to consider," Jan said.

"Only madmen would convince their people that a cure is a poison," Pavel said.

"The world is full of madmen," Jan said.

"I think only of the lives that could be saved," Pavel said, and hung his head.

Jan sighed, and said, "First, we have to find the book. Second, we don't know if there is anything in the book about curing any illness. Third, we will decide what to do with it once we see what the pages contain."

Pavel nodded, and Jan began working on deciphering a 13th letter.

17

EMAUSKLOSTER 1943

IT WAS THE second Sunday of Advent, and Roman stood alone lighting a purple candle in a wreath at the Imperial Chapel's altar. He stepped back, and softly sang, "*Veni, Redemptor Gentium*." When he finished, he heard a voice behind him.

"What is that song? I think I know it in German," Renate said.

"It's just a hymn. One that has always brought me comfort," Roman said. "Have you come to pray?"

"Yes," she said. "And to say hello. Why are these pews moved here in the back?"

"Meinrer's men, searching for the book," Roman said, shaking his head.

"The power of books," Renate said.

"What?" Roman asked.

Renate said, "Books. There is something about

them. When I was a girl, we had little. We had more than some of our neighbors, but our dinners were mostly potato soup. Still, we had a small library of books, and I suggested we sell some of them. My mother scolded me."

"Why?" Roman asked.

"She said one must never sell a book, because you can never get its true value in the exchange. That even a dusty book you have not touched in years is worth much more than the money someone is willing to pay for it," Renate said.

"Can one never give a book as a gift then? And are they too valuable to lend?" Roman asked.

"To give a book is a dear gift, and personal in selecting the title, but she also said to never lend a book. Give a person a book, or do not, but do not lend," Renate said.

Just then, another of the nurses came in. She was stern, with a severe face and her hair tied tightly back.

"Frau Ritschel," Renate said.

"What are you doing in here?" Ritschel asked.

"I came to pray. I hoped the brother would be here, and he is. Brother Roman, this is Frau Gertrud Ritschel, the nurse supervisor," Renate said.

"Have you finished the work I gave you to do?" Ritschel asked.

"I have," Renate said.

"Perhaps we should find you some more, to keep

you busy," Ritschel said, looking first at Renate, and then at Roman.

"To keep her too busy to pray?" Roman asked.

"What?" Ritschel asked. Renate looked at the floor.

"Are you opposed to this young woman spending time in prayer?" Roman asked.

"Do not interfere. You are not even a priest. I would speak to Herr Meinrer about you, if you do not hold your tongue. You could end up dead in a camp, like your friends," Ritschel said.

Renate looked up at Ritschel, and Roman stepped forward. He asked, "Who is dead?"

Ritschel shrugged, and said, "All of them. Vykoup, and the other priests and monks from this place, all of them."

"It can't be. Why, in these days, would an army make war on peaceful men of God? The Holy Father has no army. There is nothing to be gained," Roman said.

"There is much to be lost by resisting," Ritschel said.

"Monsters," Renate whispered.

Roman knelt, and sat on his heels. He lowered his head and said, "*Majko Bozja, moliza nas grješnike…*"

"What was that?" Ritschel asked.

"Czech praying," Renate said softly.

"That was not Czech," Ritschel said.

Roman said nothing and remained as he was. Renate approached him, and extended one arm as if to touch his shoulder, but then Ritschel said, "Come away from there. Leave him to his praying."

Renate hesitated until Ritschel hissed at her, and then Renate turned on the older woman and said, "Go on, you old witch. He's lost the only family he had. I'll stay with him."

Ritschel took a step backward, a shocked expression on her face, but then her jaw reset. She turned and stormed off.

Roman remained on his knees.

"Brother, are you praying? If so, would you like to move to a pew?" Renate asked, touching Roman's shoulder. He looked up at her. Renate touched his face, and caressed it. Roman stared up at her. He remembered the brothers, the abbot, and others he'd lost over the years. Roman knew that he had to find the book, and to protect both book and journal from the Nazis.

"I could pray with you," Renate offered.

Roman looked at the floor, drew a deep breath, and stood. He took Renate's hand, and led her to the pew nearest the altar, where he sat and pulled her down beside him. Reaching into his robe, he pulled out the journal.

"I've been working on this. This was written by a monk, long ago, who was translating the very book for which Meinrer is searching. These are his notes," Roman said, flipping through the pages.

"There is more writing in there," Renate said.

"The original author used a cypher to encrypt his

notes, and these are the notes of another monk who broke the code, including where the book was hidden," Roman said.

"Let's go get it!" Renate said.

"The book is no longer there; both the original notes and the first decryption happened almost 600 years ago," Roman said.

"So, what is there left for you to work on?" Renate asked.

"A few decades after the original journal was written, and the book was discovered and rehidden, someone else came by this journal. A Hussite named Vaclav. He also found and read the book, and then hid it once more, adding new encrypted notes. Mercifully, there is much less to decode, but his encryption was far more sophisticated than the one used by Som Zec," Roman said.

"Who was Som?" she asked.

"It was originally his journal. He was one of the most famous translators ever to work in this place," Roman said.

Renate stared at the journal, and then said, "If it has stayed hidden for more than 500 years, you should leave it and flee this monastery. It is only a matter of time before Meinrer will send you somewhere dreadful, or kill you outright."

"I cannot. The Germans are being too thorough. Although I do not know where the book is, this is not that big a place. I know of secret corners, and even rooms, but Meinrer and his men will find even those eventually," Roman said.

"What then?" she asked.

"I will finish breaking the Hussite's code, find the book, and either take it from here, or burn it. Perhaps it should have been burned long ago," Roman said.

"What is in the book?" Renate asked. She stared, eyes wet, waiting for an answer.

Roman looked as if he might answer, but then said, "Whatever is in the book, Meinrer and the Nazis must never have it."

Renate said nothing, but reached and caressed his face once more. Roman closed his eyes at the touch, and leaned into her hand. She took his face into both of her hands, and Roman opened his eyes. They were wet, and he searched her face for some sign. She leaned closer, and then so did he. Their mouths were inches apart, when Roman suddenly withdrew.

Renate stood, and said, "I am sorry. I did not mean to do that to you, to tempt you."

Roman rose, put his hand on her arm, and said, "We are just people. There was no sin, no wrongdoing in the eyes of God."

"But devotion, piety, your vow of chastity," Renate said.

"Promises created by men who never followed them, and sworn to by men who should not have. Christ's original message was of acceptance, suffrage, and love," Roman said, taking hold of both of her arms.

"I don't understand," she said.

"Now is not the time, and this is not the place. Perhaps later, and elsewhere," Roman said.

They stared silently into each other's eyes, until Renate said, "Perhaps in the new year," and smiled.

Roman nodded.

"So, you will work on the Hussite's notes?" she asked.

"And when I believe I know where to look, I will go find the book," he said.

"Take me with you when you do," Renate said.

Roman smiled a bit, but said nothing.

"I should leave, before Ritschel comes looking for me again," Renate said, and then they embraced in a hug. "Please be careful," she said.

"I will," Roman said.

Without looking into his face again, Renate let him go and left. Roman went to his cell with the journal, and turned to Vaclav the Hussite's notes.

18

EMAUZY
2022

VISITORS WERE WELCOME in the monastery and, as they came in, there was a table to their right with a scale model of the building itself, and beyond that, a counter where they could pay a small fee to visit. Tourists had not really found Emauzy monastery yet, but every once in a while, a person or two would come in, wander the hallways, admiring and photographing the centuries-old frescoes on the ceilings.

As Christophe was coming back in, carrying a bag of fruit from market, he noticed that on the table was an envelope, marked simply, "Rossignol." He picked it up, turning it over, looking for something more, but there was nothing.

He took the fruit and the envelope to their workspace, and found her already at work on the copies of the journal.

"This was left for you in the *vstup*," he said.

She took it, her brow a bit furrowed, and opened it. She sighed.

"What is it?" Christophe asked.

She handed it to him. It was written in French, but clearly not by a native speaker. It read, "You must stop looking for the book. This is your final warning. You will absolutely NOT be allowed to make its contents public…"

Christophe asked, "How does he know what the contents of the book even are?"

"He doesn't," she said, without looking up.

Christophe continued to read, "It would be a catastrophe. The purported contents could tear down social structures and rituals that have existed for millennia. Structures upon which not only religion depend, but which act as the models for governments, and even families. You believe you hunt for the truth, but it is a book of lies, designed to destroy everything. You are being watched. You are warned. Halt your searching for the book. Halt!"

"We're being watched?" Christophe asked.

"Apparently so. It must be a very boring exercise. We spend our days working in here, and sleep in quarters within these walls. So far, their surveillance has likely only determined information such as what type of fruit you bought today," she said.

"They would also know that a detective visited.

Maybe that is helpful. Do you really think it is Tiwari?" he asked.

"It doesn't really matter to me," she said.

"It could be Sabatini, or Morris," he said.

"Let's get to work, yes?"

"Why did you say 'they'? Do you suspect it is more than one?" he asked.

"He. They. Whatever. Get to work," she said.

"I prefer 'he,' as in one, solo," he said.

She only nodded and hummed in response. He sat at his desk, and began reading and scribbling notes on the photocopies of the journal.

They worked into the evening, and had only some of Christophe's fruit for dinner.

"These marks. It really seems as though someone else has already decoded the Hussite's notes. I wish he had included the translation in these pages. This could take weeks. We're not cryptologists," Christophe said.

"Perhaps they were working in a time when they didn't feel particularly safe," she said.

"The Nazi occupation? Do you think these notes are so recent?" Christophe asked.

"Perhaps," she said. "The few words the most recent translator wrote here and there are in Czech, and not in German. So, it's either relatively recent or quite old. I think it's the former."

The door opened before the person began knocking. Both Professor Rossignol and Christophe covered their work, but when she saw it was Brother Antonin, she relaxed.

"So glad you could come, but I thought we said afternoon? I think we could use your help with these, but it is a bit late," she said, rubbing her eyes.

"He knows?" Christophe asked.

Antonin and Professor Rossignol both looked at Christophe for a moment, and then she said, "Christophe, Brother Antonin is the source of these pages."

"We have you to thank," Christophe said. "Have you tried to break the Hussite's code?"

"I have. I must say, I'm not sure that his notes will lead you to the manuscript you seek," Antonin.

"Then why give us the pages?" Christophe asked.

"When the professor asked if I had anything that might be connected to the manuscript, I gave her these," Antonin said.

"And how did you come by them?" Christophe asked.

"I've had them for some time; they were left to me by an elder. To be honest, I had misplaced them for a time, but was lucky enough to find them again. Still, I do not know how much the pages will help," he said.

"Perhaps the two of you can find something, but I think I've done all I can today," she said, standing. "I'll return to it in the morning. Good evening to you both."

"Goodnight, professor," Christophe said, rising. Antonin only bowed slightly, and watched her leave.

Both men then sat opposite each other, on either side of Christophe's desk.

There were a few moments of silence, but then Christophe cut right to the chase, and said, "Do you really believe the secret book still exists, if it ever did?"

"I certainly believe it did exist, and it likely still does. People, with a few historical exceptions, hate to destroy books. They are horrified when others do it. Demolish a building, and many people see it as making way for something new. Destroy any sort of creative work, such as a painting, and people will be sad, or perhaps angry, but it is not the same as a book. A painting of an event may contain a few stories, and perhaps a half-dozen unanswered questions, but a book—it can contain thousands of inquiries combined with the tensions of each having multiple possible outcomes. When a book is destroyed, so much is lost," Antonin said.

"But you do not believe these notes will lead us to the current location of the book. Why not? What is in the Hussite's notes?" Christophe asked.

"It has been centuries since those notes were written," Antonin said.

"And a good portion of this place was rebuilt after the stupid mistake by the Americans, so perhaps the book was destroyed or discovered," Christophe said.

Antonin winced, paused, and then said, "If the book had been discovered, we would know."

"Because of its contents," Christophe said.

Antonin said, "Throughout the history of Emauzy, of this place, words and manuscripts have come and gone. Learned men have spent their lives translating and illuminating documents. Even Jan Hus spared this place, and the monks in it. Still, many have been tortured and killed over ideas put down in ink. The Nazis sent the abbot and most of the monks to die in a concentration camp."

"I read that, too, but not that it was because of a book. The Nazis sent many priests to the camps. That is not unique to the history of this place," Christophe said.

Antonin ignored him and said, "Sharing new ideas has always carried some risk. Even some of those who came to destroy the truth, or steal it, have met with disaster."

"Are you warning us? You've heard of the threats?" Christophe asked.

"I have heard the histories, and lost people myself in this war," Antonin said.

"War?" Christophe asked.

"There have been wars fought over land, treasure, or resources…to set people free or to enslave others. There have been wars fought in response to mere insults. Still, there is a war that never stops. Sometimes there is bloodshed, and sometimes pauses in the violence, but the war that never ends is the war to control the narrative. Those that control the narrative can explain away the vilest actions, and the worst deprivations. The war over the narrative has always been the key to everything," Antonin said.

"And the hidden book is important in that war?" Christophe asked.

"In the world, there are a few texts that have been used as rationalization for the actions of one group or another, and even certain members within a group, to anoint themselves as the righteous. They construct complex webs of support for their actions, their decisions, and proclaim themselves not only uniquely qualified to interpret the holy documents of whatever religion, but even to have the right to add to them. New laws, new rituals, new restrictions, new denials of access, and new exclusions. The book you seek strips much of the complications away from one of the most important of those texts," Antonin said, and then added, "Or so they say."

"Do these people also think themselves so special that they have the right to hide these texts?" Christophe asked.

Antonin froze for a moment, and then said, "Some do think it is time for the secrets of the book you seek to be revealed." He leaned back in his chair, closed his eyes, and sighed. When he opened them again, he asked, "Can I see the progress you are making?"

Christophe reached over to the edge of his desk,

grabbed a few photocopied pages, and handed them over. He said, "I've got pieces of it broken out here."

Antonin took these, began to scan them, and then nodded as if confirming. He said nothing.

Christophe looked at the monk for a moment longer, and then returned to the work directly in front of him. As the hours passed, his eyes grew heavy. Reading, cross-referencing, and scribbling, he worked, growing more and more weary, until he fell asleep on his desk, with his cheek on his work.

19

MONASTERY OF THE SLAVS
1373

JAN DID NOT dip into the ink again. He only stared at the last notation he had made in Som's journal.

Pavel asked, "All these notes about the translation, pages and pages, but that is all it says of the hiding place?"

Jan said, "That is all of it. Do you know what it could mean?"

"Why didn't the old man simply say where it was?" Pavel asked.

Jan, reading aloud, said, "Beneath a hole, where the sun shines on the fat, I leave this each day."

"He buried it. Surely inside the walls, but we would see this," Pavel said.

Jan said, "But fat? We pour the rancid fat outdoors."

Pavel said, "But the weather would destroy the book, in any hole outside."

Jan said, "So, under floor stones, but not in the hidden rooms. There is no sunshine in those."

"So then under a floor we see every day? Impossible," Pavel said.

"We are not understanding its full meaning. What of the fat?" Jan asked.

Pavel stood, and paced a few steps, "The idiot. Why did he do this? Why not simply tell where to find it? He must have known you would be the one to read it if he were not able." He was clearly becoming angry.

Jan moved to his bed, and lay across it.

"You would sleep?" Pavel asked.

Jan said, "I am only resting a moment, and thinking. Old Som was no idiot. If he intended for me, or anyone, to find the book, he expected this riddle to be understood."

"He was an idiot, and I think him selfish. He is mocking us with this," Pavel said.

"Sit, calm yourself," Jan said, opening his eyes, but not rising.

"I will not. I have had enough of all of this foolishness," Pavel said, and left the cell.

"Wait, Pavel," Jan called after him, but he was gone. Jan closed his eyes once more, and thought about holes, sunlight, and fat. He felt the answer was there, and he knew that Som would have put it within his power to decipher it. However, it was not long before Jan fell asleep. When he woke, it was almost dark outside. Looking at his small table, he saw that it was gone. Everything else was there, but Som Zec's journal was missing.

Jan searched his cell, and then again, and then he realized that Pavel must have returned and taken it. Walking down the corridor toward Pavel's cell, Jan caught a glimpse of him turning the corner ahead. Jan hurried and followed him, and watched as he went into the refectory.

Peeking in through the door, he could see Pavel was working to free a stone at the base of the window farthest from the entrance. Jan stepped inside, and said, "Pavel, what are you doing?"

Pavel spun to face him. "I understand it! It was not a hole in the floor! It is a hole in the wall, a window!"

Jan said, "But there are many windows here."

"Jan! Brother Jiri sat here, and the sun from this window always shone on him," Pavel said.

Jiri was, by far, the fattest of the monks. "Such a childish clue?"

Pavel said, "He was leaving it for you, after all," but he did not smile. Instead, he turned and began to try to wrest free the first stone beneath the window.

"That stone goes completely through the wall. You will never…"

Just then, the stone came free, and was less than a third as large as Jan had expected. Pavel carelessly dropped the stone, and reached into the space from where it had come. His hands shaking, he pulled the leather-covered book from the wall. The same that Jan had seen Som Zec receive from the Regensburg monk.

"You have it!" Jan said.

"Soon, everyone will have it," Pavel said.

"What?"

"We will give it to everyone. We will make transcriptions and share this with everyone. These damn secrets! Always about secrets, the power of secrets, the power of withholding the truth!" Pavel said.

"Old Som was willing to die to protect it! We should learn what is in it first, and then bring it to learned monks to decide. It may not be hidden truths, but instead dangerous lies," Jan said.

"We will let the secrets out. The answer to the plague is in here, I can feel it," Pavel said.

"How can you know that?" Jan said, walking toward him.

"Stay away! You would take this from me, and I will not let you!" Pavel said. He was sweating profusely.

Jan stopped. "What is wrong with you? You are acting as if you have gone mad. This is not like you. We can translate it first, and then decide what to do with it."

"Ah but that is just like you! You have always liked it here, the apprentice to old Som. Favored by so many. You came here of your own volition! Not me. I was abandoned here! To atone for shameful family secrets that I still know nothing about, but I…I was the offering. 'Offer up your third son to God and all will be forgiven.' Well, I have not forgiven! And now I need something for myself," Pavel said.

"What? What do you need? The book?" Jan asked.

Pavel lifted his tunic, exposing a large, black sore on his upper thigh. "The pestilencia has come for me! And this book will be my salvation from it!"

Jan raised his hands, and said, "Pavel, if it is in there, we will find it together. Just calm yourself."

"I cannot be calm! I have a day or two to live! Days to pry from this book what I need!"

Jan stepped closer, and said, "You are my friend. Let me help you."

Pavel moved quickly to the large hearth, with the fire burning low inside. "If I cannot have it, no one will!"

"Pavel, you were just saying its secrets need to be revealed! Be calm. I am still your friend," Jan said.

Pavel shouted, "I see it in your face! You see me as dead already, and you would take this from me!"

Pavel had clearly been driven mad by all of this. Jan stepped closer, and Pavel raised his hand as if to throw the book into the flames. Leaping forward, Jan got his hands on the book, and Pavel clubbed him hard in the ear. Jan pushed Pavel with the book, knocking him to the ground, and freeing it from his grasp. Pavel sprang to his feet and leapt at Jan, and both monks went to the floor. Jan could feel how Pavel was burning with fever. Pavel hit Jan, again and again, and Jan could scarcely defend himself while gripping the book with both hands. Both of them were still on the floor, and Jan pushed Pavel away enough to get to his feet. He turned to run with the book, to hide it elsewhere, but then heard Pavel pull a torch from the wall. Its flames smoked at the end of the meter-long rod.

"I will burn it right out of your hands!" Pavel said.

"Stop this!" Jan said, backing slowly.

Pavel lunged, missed the book, and instead the torch's lit end struck Jan on the side of his neck, the soft skin immediately blistering and rupturing. Jan screamed and ran. He could hear Pavel following as Jan passed through the doorway to the garth. As Pavel came out, he stumbled and fell. The torch flew, and fell harmlessly on the stones, out of reach.

Pavel lay on his side, and began to cry. Jan tucked the book inside his robes, touched Pavel's face, and felt once more the fever raging within him. Pavel's sobs turned to coughs and choking. Jan picked up his friend, and carried him to his cell. Once there, he pulled Pavel's robes away, and tried to cool him with water.

Pavel regained consciousness only once in the night, said nothing that Jan could understand, and died before sunrise, his fever having never broken. The burn on Jan's neck was excruciating, and he needed to make a salve for himself, but first he would see to his friend.

Jan washed Pavel's body, carried him out to the graveyard, and buried him close to Som Zec. He prayed for as long as he could stand the pain.

Making himself a quick salve for his burn, Jan placed it carefully on his neck. It stung as it went on. He had been told that the salve was not intended for an open wound, but more for blistered skin, but he didn't know what else to do.

After this, he went to the refectory, replacing the unlit torch in its place, and returning the stone beneath the window. Jan went next to Pavel's cell to look for Som Zec's journal, but could not find it. Returning to his own cell, he pulled the book from his robes.

20

EMAUSKLOSTER 1944

ROMAN STOOD UP, and quickly tore a few pages out of the journal he'd been working on for weeks. Moving to one corner of his cell, he knelt, and slid them into a space between two stones in his wall. Standing once more, and satisfied that the pages could not be seen, he grabbed and wadded up his notes. These he set alight, and watched as they quickly burned. The air in the small room was fouled, but he didn't care. Roman, still holding the journal, minus the pages he'd removed, went to find Renate.

He looked in where the other nurses were congregated, saw the other women, including Nurse Ritschel who scowled at him, but not Renate. Roman continued to search, and found Renate outside in the garth. As he stepped out into the chill and dark, he could make out more her silhouette than her facial features.

"What are you doing out here?" Roman asked.

"I wanted some fresh air," she said.

"You don't even have a coat," he said.

She just stared at the sky, until she said, "I was hoping to see the stars but there are too many clouds. Almost like fog. Strange for February, don't you think?"

Roman said, "Renate, I've learned where the book is. Come on."

"You've found it?" she asked, following him to the door and back into the hallway.

"I have learned where Vaclav hid it. There is no way to know if it is still there without going to look," he said.

"Think we should?" she asked.

"Most of the soldiers are in their quarters. There are only the couple guards still awake and walking the hallways. Let's go," Roman said.

Renate nodded, and they walked quickly down the hall and around the first corner.

"Where are we going?" she asked.

"The refectory," Roman said.

"It's in there?"

"It is under the hearth," Roman said.

"We'll never be able to lift that!"

He said, "We won't have to."

They walked into the refectory, and went to the massive hearth stone. Kneeling beside the front right corner, they felt the warmth of the fire on their skin, and Roman began to work to free a much smaller tile beside it.

"That tile has not been there for centuries," Renate said.

"True, but wait a moment," he said. The tile came up, and he set it aside. Then Roman began to dig down and underneath the corner of the hearth stone. There were more small stones beneath it, forming a small wall beneath the corner of the hearth, and working one of these smaller ones loose, he revealed a space. Reaching in, he pulled out a leather-covered book.

"Oh my God, is that it?" Renate asked.

Roman nodded, rubbing the cover with his hand.

"Open it!" she said.

The city's air raid sirens began to sound, something that had not happened often in Prague.

Roman looked up, and said, "Not yet," and instead, he hid the book inside his robes.

"An air raid?" she asked, looking up at the ceiling.

"I'll hide this in there for now, and we can leave this place," he said, holding up the remaining journal.

Just then, there came a voice from behind them. It was Nurse Ritschel, who said, "See, I told you."

Stepping out from behind Ritschel was Hauptsturmführer Meinrer, a pistol in his hand, and from behind him, two armed soldiers. He had his uniform pants and boots, but he was wearing a simple cotton shirt. It seemed clear that he had rushed from his quarters when Nurse Ritschel had gone to get him.

"No need to hide anything," Meinrer said.

Meinrer and the two soldiers came forward, but Nurse Ritschel stayed near the door. "Give us the book," Meinrer said, pointing at the journal with his pistol. The air raid sirens continued to sound, but Meinrer seemed completely unconcerned.

Roman began to hand the journal to him, but then tossed it into the fire, and shouted, "Run!"

Meinrer shouted, "Save the book!" He and the soldiers did not initially try to stop Roman or Renate as they ran for the door, but instead concentrated on trying to rescue what they thought was the book. As they passed Nurse Ritschel, Renate backhanded the woman in the side of her head.

Roman and Renate sprinted down the hallway. When he stopped suddenly, he had to grab her arm. She didn't know about the hiding spaces.

"What are you doing? They're coming!" she said.

Roman slid sideways into a dark space in the wall, and said, "Follow!"

"There's no room in there for us!" she said.

"Trust me!" he said, and saw her following.

"We are going to get stuck," she said.

"Be silent and follow," he said, and then in the dark the space suddenly widened. He held out his hand and, as she came into the small windowless chamber, she walked into his outstretched hand. He felt her grip his arm, and heard her say, "It's a secret room."

"Shhh," Roman said, and even with the air raid sirens, they soon heard the soldiers run right past them.

"Are there many of these spaces?" she asked.

"Several," he said. "There is a small bench here. Let's sit for a moment."

The air raid sirens stopped, and it was suddenly very quiet in the darkness.

21

EMAUZY
2022

WHEN CHRISTOPHE WOKE, the office was awash in early morning daylight, and he was momentarily disoriented. He looked at the windows, his desk, his clothes, and then at Antonin, who was sitting across the room, watching him.

"You're still here?" Christophe asked.

"What is the difference? Go back to my quarters, or simply stay here. I'd likely lie awake in either place, considering the ramifications of you finding the actual book," he said.

"Do you know where it is? Why toy with us if you do?" Christophe asked, still rubbing the sleep from his eyes, and somewhat embarrassed by the drool spot on the photocopies.

"Believe me, nothing about this is a game," Antonin said. He stood and slowly walked toward Christophe.

It wasn't menacing, but each step seemed important, requiring effort, until he stopped inches from the other side of Christophe's desk.

"What is it?" Christophe asked.

"Are you sure you want to find the book? Even if your life is never the same again? Or the professor's? Even if finding it means you will change the lives of so many devoted people, and rewrite history? Turn heroes into villains, and to cause the disgraced to be honored? There are be many who will hate you for it," Antonin asked.

Christophe looked him in the eyes, and knew that he had to find the book. "Where is it, Antonin?"

There was a sudden, sharp knock at the door. Antonin wheeled around just as Detective Potok entered with another policeman.

"I thought as much," Potok said. "Brother Antonin, or whoever you are, you are being detained."

"Wait! Why are you doing this?" Christophe said.

Just then, Professor Rossignol walked into the room, looking stunned, and asked, "What is happening?"

"While investigating those threats made against you, I made an interesting discovery about the good Brother here," Potok said.

"But he's been helping us," the professor said.

"He's not the one," Christophe said as Potok placed handcuffs on Antonin, who did not resist in the least.

"That may be, but there is no official record of

this man, of this monk named Antonin, before he was nineteen years old. He has no birth records, no identification documents before he was a grown man, nothing. So, he may be innocent, but we will detain him until we can get some idea of who he is," Potok said.

"But this is ridiculous. Detective, you must investigate Anil Tiwari, he is the most likely suspect," Christophe said, as he came around the desk.

"We are following every lead, including this one," Potok said.

Christophe's eyes met Antonin's, and the monk leaned a bit closer, and said quietly, "Check the tower, the astrological tower, in the Klementinum. Look for a thin, brown leather-bound book, between two fat books bound in red."

"Come on," Potok said, pulling Antonin away.

"You have seen it recently? No one is allowed in there," Christophe said.

"What did he say?" asked the professor.

Detective Potok, the police officer, and Antonin were suddenly gone, and Christophe turned to Professor Rossignol and said, "I think I know where the book is."

"Where?" she asked.

"The Klementinum," he said.

"All this time, it's been hidden among academics, and not the clergy?" she asked.

Christophe nodded, and said, "If he was telling the truth."

"Let's go," she said.

"Let me go. If I find it, I'll come straight back. If something goes wrong, one of us should be around to explain what we are working on," he said.

"How could something go that wrong?" she asked.

"Antonin did not make those threats," Christophe said. "That person is still out there."

"Take policemen with you," she said.

"It will take months to get permission to get into that library," he said.

"You think it's in the actual Klementinum library?"

"It must be," Christophe said.

"Well, you cannot break in. You have to pay to get in. They give tours. A guide stands in the door to prevent anyone from entering. Even taking photographs of the library from the hallway is forbidden," she said.

"Professor, I know all this," he said.

"What will you do?"

"I'll figure it out as I go. I'm going there right now," Christophe said. "I'll come right back here."

"Unless you are arrested," she said.

"Yes, unless that," he said, and then he left the office, and went back through the *vstup*. Once outside, he made his way up the hill to the nearby tram stop. Riding the tram, his heart was racing. Not at the thought that he might end up in jail, but the idea that he was about to put his hands on a book that so many had sought out.

Once off the tram, he walked to the little courtyard, and the nondescript door with the small sign that was the entrance to the tower. He bought a ticket for a tour, but then did not wait for one. Christophe had taken the tour years before, as a tourist on his first trip to Prague. He passed through a couple doors as if he belonged there, and the few people standing around said nothing to him. He began ascending stairs that looked more like they were constructed in the 1960s than the 1690s. The walls were white, the stairs looked industrial and spiraled their way up.

Christophe heard then what he thought were someone else's footfalls on the steps beneath him. He stopped, and listened. Nothing. He began to climb again, and finally reaching the top, passed through a plain door. It was a dead-end hallway, with historical displays in glass cases, and also a copy of the Vyšehrad Codex, an illuminated text of some size, replicated so that visitors could actually page through it.

At the far end, on the left, was the famous library. He made his way to the entrance, and as he approached, he saw the doors were open. He couldn't believe his luck, until a tour guide stepped out of the library and into his path.

"Sir, you know you cannot enter the library, I'm sure," the guide said.

"I know, thank you," Christophe said.

"There will be a tour in twenty-five minutes, if you would like," he said.

"Thank you," Christophe said again.

The guide turned and locked the doors to the library. The thought flashed through Christophe's mind of attempting to take the key by force, but the guide had at least thirty pounds on him, and Christophe had never been in a physical fight in his life. The guide walked away without another word, and when the hallway door closed, Christophe was alone. He looked at the locked doors to the library, and knew if he so much as rattled the handle, police would come rushing to the tower. He looked up at a surveillance camera, likely one of a dozen monitored by a bored employee, but still there to provide evidence at his future trial that he had broken into a world-famous and ancient library.

Christophe walked backwards, meaning to lean with his back on the wall, when he bumped into a glass display. It was an octagonal cylinder, taller than Christophe, with several shelves. Behind its glass he could see books, standing upright, some of them open to be viewed. As he stepped away from it, he saw them. On the bottom shelf were two fat red books, and between those, a narrow brown leather book. Hidden in plain sight, in a display of books the caretakers did not even care if they were exposed to sunlight. More decoration than anything else, and yet the book was there, just as Antonin had said.

He looked at the closed door that led out of the small hallway. The octagonal display opened at each shelf, but Christophe did not know if it was tied into the alarm system. The book was right there, though, and he made up his mind to take it. He was not planning to sell it, or harm it. He'd gladly give it back. He hoped that the authorities would keep that in mind. There was a chance that the authorities had no idea that brown book had been inserted into their display.

Christophe decided it was worth it. He dropped to one knee, and quickly popped the glass for the bottom shelf open. Taking the book, he slipped it into his shirt, pressed the red cover volumes together, and closed the glass. He stood, and was jogging toward the door, when it flew open. Professor Ottavio Sabatini came through it.

"It was you," Christophe said.

"I warned you and the professor, more than once, to abandon this search," he said.

"You knew where it was?"

"I followed you here. The way you hurried to the tram, and then off of it to this place. I knew you were after it. You just confirmed that you found it," Sabatini said, stepping closer to Christophe, who slowly backed away.

"I couldn't get it. The library is locked," Christophe said.

"Then why were you running? Give it to me," Sabatini said. The man Christophe had always seen as a portly academic actually loomed large now, tall and menacing. He backed up again.

"But, I told you, I don't have it," Christophe said.

Sabatini struck Christophe, quickly but lightly, in what would've been his chest, but instead, he hit the book under the shirt.

"Give it to me," he said.

"Go to hell," Christophe said, trying to sound tougher than he felt.

Sabatini lunged at him, grabbing hold of Christophe's shirt, and pulling at it. The men spun, holding onto each other's clothing. Christophe was beginning to wonder if perhaps the surveillance camera might be a help to him, when he realized his foot was between Sabatini's huge feet. Bringing his knee up as hard as he could, Sabatini groaned, released Christophe's shirt, and crumpled to the floor, falling against the locked library doors. An alarm sounded, and Christophe quickly went out the hallway door and onto the stairwell. He heard footsteps below, rushing up, so he climbed and found himself in the top of the tower, and stepping out onto the balcony that went around the structure. The previous tour was still up there, and he calmly stepped in with them.

Their guide did not notice, but he did hear the alarm, and said, "Ladies and gentlemen, please wait here a moment." He called downstairs, and spoke to someone in Czech.

Christophe felt the weight of the book against his skin, its leather cover was unusually warm. He looked out over the entire city of Prague, out over the river, and up to the castle. He saw, in the distance, the churches and cathedrals. The centuries of labor to build them, the treasure spent erecting them, the bloodshed and terror ordered by the same men who had ordered their construction, but also the peace and solace the spaces had provided, the splendor and inspiration they have given. Christophe clutched the book to his chest, looked skyward, and said, "Let me share whatever is in this."

The guide turned to the group and said, "It is all fine now. Apparently, someone tried the doors to the library, but he is in custody now and has been removed. This concludes the tour. If I could ask you to head back down the way you came, and I hope you enjoy your stay here in Prague."

Christophe made his way down, to the street, and back onto the tram without incident. He was more afraid now than he had been while grappling with Sabatini. All he wanted was to be able to hand the book over to Professor Rossignol.

Walking into Emauzy, he realized that in taking the book and returning it to the monastery, he had become part of its history, and he suddenly felt a crushing unworthiness. Quickly walking to the office, he found her at her desk.

"Ah thank goodness," she said.

"I have it," he said, pulled it from his shirt, and handed it to her.

"So, no trouble then?"

"There was some trouble, yes," he said. "We should copy it quickly. And read it."

22

MONASTERY OF THE SLAVS 1373

JAN OPENED THE book, and saw that it was, in fact, written in Glagolitic. A note, apparently from the translator, said that it came from a far older text, written in Koine Greek.

Jan wished it were still in Greek. It would have been easier for him to read. Turning another page, he came to the actual beginning of the translation. It was immediately apparent that it was a firsthand account, by someone named Judas.

Jan read—

Judas the Twin, or in Aramaic—Tau'ma.
I am called Thomas, and perhaps known
best for doubt born of grief.

Sitting back, Jan said, "It cannot be. An account from the Apostle, St. Thomas?"

Jan read on. The narrator explained that when he was thirteen years old, travelers with brightly died robes, monks, arrived from the east. They appeared before King Herod, and asked for a guide to lead them to a child they believed was their reincarnated teacher. It seemed to those present that the child was in Bethlehem. Herod offered them Thomas as a guide, since he was a mere stoneworker and not a soldier, and would raise no concern among the local people. So, Thomas came to lead these men from the east to Bethlehem.

Jan paused, thinking, "Can this be authentic? Clearly someone thought enough of it to translate it, and monks have died protecting it."

He continued to read. Thomas led the eastern monks to Bethlehem, and to the house of Joseph and Mary. Inside, they found children as well. Girls and two boys. The younger of the two boys was about two years old. The older was named James, and the younger was Jesus. The monks tested young Jesus by opening a bundle of cloth on the floor. Within, there were many things. Wooden toys, bells, a knife, a gold cup, and a bronze bowl. They spread the items evenly. The boy went directly to the gold cup, lifting it into the air with both hands. By choosing this item, Jesus convinced the monks that the soul of their deceased teacher had returned to Earth and was born as Jesus. They promised to return when the boy reached manhood and invite him to come east, and study with them. That night, the monks and Thomas camped outside of the village, and Thomas had a dream warning them that Herod would kill the boy. When he told the monks, and later Joseph, about his dream, they all left Bethlehem, but, at first, without Thomas, who thought he could buy them time to escape if he returned to Jerusalem. He later caught up with them, but met a stranger, perhaps a demon, on the way. When Joseph took his family to Egypt, Thomas chose instead to go with the monks, by sea, to their homeland.

Incredible, thought Jan. Thomas had met Jesus as a young child, and testified that he had siblings! The wise men were monks, and Jesus wasn't a newborn at the time of the visit. And it was Thomas's dream, not Joseph's, that warned the holy family that they should flee. Still, except for the claim that Jesus had stepbrothers and stepsisters, the Church would likely simply mock the rest of the account.

Jan read on. The narrator, Thomas, recounted that more than ten years later, he returned to Jerusalem, and sent word to Jesus and his family to come and join him. After the family arrived, he wrote, he could see that Joseph was in poor health, and that Jesus and his brothers were all taller than Mary.

Plural! Brothers! Jan stopped reading. Clearly into sacrilege now. Should he keep reading? Was there a risk to his own soul simply by continuing?

Anxiously, he read on. Thomas wrote that James had grown into a young man, and that Jesus had younger brothers named Joses, Judas, and Simon. His sisters were Salome and Mary, but they were not dressed as Essenes as his mother Mary was. These were her stepdaughters. Thomas's account asserted that while some thought Joseph was an Essene, this was not the case. His children who were older than Jesus were not of that sect, and were the children of his first wife. Those who were younger, were the product of Joseph and Mary's union.

Jan crossed himself. If this author lived today, Jan thought, he would certainly face dire consequences. He would not be safe anywhere in Christendom.

Reading on, Jan found that Thomas claimed to discuss the past years of Jesus's youth with him and his family. A report that Jesus struck one of his teachers dead, and then restored him. Another that a snake that bit James nearly killed him, until Jesus healed his brother by breathing on the wound, and the snake burst into pieces. Still another, that while playing with Jesus on a rooftop, a child named Zenon fell and was killed. Before Jesus had even descended, Zenon's parents accused Jesus of pushing his friend off. Jesus came to Zenon's side, and restored him to life. And yet another story of life after death, bringing back a baby of nursing age.

Jan read the account of young Jesus causing elders

to marvel in the Temple, and then soon after, Thomas asked if Jesus would return with him to the east. Despite the fact that Jesus's family did not want him to go, he did.

That explains why Jesus vanishes from the Gospels around that age, Jan thought. He continued to read.

23

EMAUSKLOSTER
1944

AS RENATE AND Roman sat together on the bench, she interrupted him, and asked, "How do you know all this? You have the book, yes, but we've been sitting in a dark room, and yet you're relaying the story as if you're reading it to me now."

Roman said nothing.

"You've read it before," she said.

Roman thought about telling her a great deal, but instead, he said, "Let me share more of the story."

Roman told her that Jesus and Thomas traveled east, overland, and met others along the way, experiencing a lot for a person Jesus's age. They continued on until they reached India, and there reunited with at least some of the monks who had first visited when Jesus was a small child, and they presented him to the priests who were to teach Jesus. As proof that it was actually he, Thomas pulled the gold cup from Jesus's things, the cup that had been used in the test that had identified Jesus as the reincarnation of their friend and teacher. Jesus learned their language by reading their scriptures and also with the help of Thomas, who had long ago learned to speak and read it. The Brahman priests then began Jesus's education in earnest, and one of the things that really stood out was how almost all of their teachings were in the form of parables, of stories. So very rarely did they ever answer a question with a straightforward answer, but instead replied with a story from which the listener could extract answers for himself.

Renate said, "Just as Jesus always taught."

"Exactly," Roman said.

"Go on," Renate said.

Roman explained that although things started very well, Jesus refused to abandon his faith in God, and he railed against the caste system, saying that even the lowest among them were equal in the eyes of God. This, of course, angered those in the highest levels of society. It was also while in India that Jesus met Mary Magdalene, and she and Jesus became friends. Jesus began preaching to the lowest caste, and this was forbidden. He did this for more than a year, at first only telling these lowest people that they were of value, but then soon he was openly criticizing the highest castes. In the coming seasons, he did far worse. There was a famine of sorts, with the lowest members of society starving, while harvesting more than enough food for the upper caste. He did not tell them to steal the food, but empowered them by telling them that while the food was not theirs, their labor was their own. He told them if the priests wouldn't share the food with them, then they should not harvest it for the priests. Soon, the priests had developed a plan to murder Jesus, so he, Thomas, and Mary Magdalene fled. After a few years of moving from place to place, they decided to return to Jerusalem.

24

EMAUZY
2022

PROFESSOR ROSSIGNOL SAID, "I won't translate aloud line by line, but let me skim and relay the gist as I go."

"Of course," Christophe said, and he listened as she summarized page after page, for hours.

They finally came to the part when Jesus's ministry began, with seeking out John the Baptist, but it was Thomas who was sent ahead to find John first, and to find Jesus's brother James as well, to prepare the way. When Thomas found the Baptist, he quickly recognized that the man had gone quite mad.

"Wait… of course, we were always taught that he was different, and energetic, full of the Holy Spirit… but mad?" Christophe asked.

Scanning ahead, she said, "The description in this text is that of a raving madman, full of faith, but driven mad by the murder of his father, the loss of his mother, and years of living off insects and tree sap."

"Honey?" Christophe asked.

"It says tree sap," she said. "May I continue?"

"Sorry, I won't interrupt."

The professor said that, according to the book, Thomas then sought out James, Jesus's elder brother, and told him Jesus would soon return. Jesus had given strict instructions however, that none of his remaining family be told. After eleven days, Jesus arrived, with Mary Magdalene riding upon an animal, which he led from the ground. After James offers Jesus the opportunity to return to building with stone, Mary tells James that they have returned to teach. James expressed his anxiety about a woman who tries to teach men. The four of them went back to see John the Baptist, and Jesus asked John to baptize him. John complied, and announced to everyone that Jesus was the one for whom he has prepared a path. And just as we've been told, Jesus met Andrew there, who promised to bring his brother and follow Jesus to Galilee.

"Actually, so far, it is not that earth-shattering. The Magdalene is more present, far more important, and the Baptist is madder than we imagined, but it is hardly the stuff that would justify murders," Christophe said.

She ignored him, and continued reading. She relayed that the text said that Andrew brought his brother Simon, and much of the narrative continues to focus on the collecting of the apostles. Philip was found, and then Nathanael bar-Talemai.

"Ah, he was a single person," Christophe said.

The professor said, "Yes, it seems Nathaniel and Bartholomew really were the same, single person." She went on reading and explained that Mary Magdalene finally met Mary, mother of Jesus, at the wedding.

"Hold on," the professor said. "He didn't turn water into wine, according to this. He recognized that the jars were not empty, but that the wine was thick in the bottom of the tall jars, and needed to be reconstituted with water. Jesus told them to fill the jars with clean water, and stir. To many of the simpler guests and servants, the water was changed into wine."

"So, this is something. If the miracles begin to get explained away like this, that would certainly be something the Church would frown upon," Christophe said.

Professor Rossignol flipped forward, read as she went, and said, "The text seems to be filled with more logical explanations for many of the mystical facets of the Gospels. Such as the temptation in the wilderness… it seems that was actually Jesus and Thomas, not Satan. Possession and driving out spirits seem to be explained by psychology. And here, it has Thomas referring to the 'lunatic Saul, remembered to be one of the Pharisees, and his journeys among the Gentiles, calling himself Paul and claiming to speak for Jesus'."

"Wow! That one would get him in trouble!" Christophe said, and he thought the professor almost smiled.

"There is mention of basic medicine in here that the three brought back from India that was still unknown to their homeland. Also, it is not Mary Magdalene who anointed his feet with oil, but Mary the sister of Lazarus, and it was Mary Magdalene, jealous of the touching, who admonished her for it, saying the oil might have been sold to feed the poor. It seems the two sisters and Lazarus were wealthy, and worldly. Mary says the oil was from the east, and Thomas reports remembering the scent from a village called Kapilavastu," the professor relayed.

"Tibet?" Christophe asked.

She continued, "Later, the sickly Lazarus takes something for his cough those assembled call 'soma' and Spikenard."

Christophe said, "Spikenard? They could only have found that above 8,000 feet in the Himalayas."

"Again, these were wealthy people. They might have had to travel as far as Damascus, or send someone there, to retrieve goods of these kinds," she said.

They went on to Judea next, the professor explained, and met Judas Iscariot. Thomas explains that he was called this because he was the son of Simon of

Kerioth. Jesus and all of his followers were baptizing others when they learned of John the Baptist's imprisonment. They all went to Jerusalem, but they knew there would be little they could do. When they got there, they learned of the Baptist's death, and it was this that enraged Jesus. This was when he fashioned a whip and drove the animals and people from the steps of the Temple, upsetting tables and spilling coins, and letting doves loose.

"That makes more sense than being angry with 'money changers.' I mean, they'd likely been there for many years, right?" Christophe asked.

Thomas wrote that Jesus was angering the priests and the high strata of society just as he had back in India. He engaged in repeated and public debates with religious authorities. He also continued to heal people, including the servant of a Roman Centurion.

"Ah! Fishes and loaves! All he did was convince the crowd to share what each had brought with them, and were hiding from each other," the professor said.

"Makes much more sense," Christophe said, and smiled. Her face looked tired, he thought, but she did not slow down, and went on to the next part.

"Here is the part about Lazarus being resurrected from the dead," she said.

"He really did that?" Christophe asked.

The professor read that Lazarus was 'as if' dead, but Jesus sent one of Lazarus's sisters to fetch hing, and

Jesus used it to revive him. "An overdose. Lazarus was unconscious from an overdose of his other drugs, and hing is an antidote," she said.

"I've never heard of it," Christophe said.

"Asafoetida," she offered.

"Ah yes," Christophe said.

"Lazarus was brought back from a drug overdose with the antidote," she said.

"No wonder monks of the 14th century who knew what was in this book were so concerned. It turns Jesus from deity into doctor," Christophe said.

"It must be more than that. It's not these miracles that make him Jesus Christ. It's the biggest miracle. The resurrection of Jesus," she said.

"Should we skip ahead?" he asked.

"There's not that much more to go," she said, and began relaying what was in the book once more, getting to the betrayal, trial, and crucifixion. It suggests that Jesus kissed Judas, that Judas was murdered, and that the crowd did not choose between two men, Jesus and Barabbas. Pilate had Jesus beaten, despite finding him innocent, and announced to the crowd his intention to release him. The crowd was not a crowd of Jews at large, but a smaller group of political priests. In fact, Thomas related that he believed if more of the common Jews had been there, Jesus would have been released. Instead, Pilate ordered him crucified at the insistence of those few present. Thomas said that after he appeared to die, they requested Jesus be taken down and turned over to his family for burial. Pilate was shocked that Jesus had died so quickly, and it was not customary to take the dead down from a cross. They usually were left to hang there for birds and animals to feed on, to serve as warnings to others, and the other two who were crucified alongside Jesus were left on their crosses, according to the book, and not taken down for the holy days to come.

"Aside from historical details, this does not erode the Church's teachings," Christophe said.

"How about this?" the professor asked, and then she explained that the book related that Jesus did not die on the cross.

"What?"

Professor Rossignol said that the book told how the body, once in the tomb, had a detectable heartbeat.

"How is this possible? He was nailed to a cross and stabbed with a spear?" Christophe said.

"Well I *am* skimming, I must have missed something," she said, paused, rubbing her eyes. "Plus, keep in mind, the whole damn thing is in Glagolitic. But according to this, once he was in the tomb, his mother placed her ear on his chest and fainted at the sound of his heartbeat."

"Then what?" Christophe asked.

Professor Rossignol said the book told how they got Jesus out of there, and moved him to the empty home of a relative. Mary Magdalene then reported to the apostles that she had seen Jesus alive. Most believed her, but Simon Peter was angry. Jesus then went to his followers, but without Thomas, whom he left at the home to protect Mary Magdalene. When Jesus returned, he sent Thomas to gauge their reactions, at which time Thomas pretended not to believe that Jesus had returned.

"Even the Doubting Thomas story turns out to be dubious," Christophe said.

The book went on to explain how Jesus sent his followers out to various destinations, even sending his mother with Philip, because his older brother, known as James the Just, was staying in Jerusalem.

She said, "It seems that Thomas and Jesus went to India, but Thomas to the far south, and Jesus to the north. The book's narrator being Thomas, much of the rest focuses on his teachings in India, and his eventual arrest. But he writes that Jesus lived out his years in northern India, and buried his mother there when she died." Professor Rossignol closed the book.

25

MONASTERY OF THE SLAVS 1373

WHEN JAN FINISHED reading the entire manuscript, he closed it, lay down on his bed, and clutched it to his chest. It was a great deal to absorb. He understood fully how dangerous and wonderful the book was, why people would die to keep the message from getting out, but also why no one would dare destroy it.

He had not eaten or had anything to drink in a long time, and his throat was parched, but his head and heart were so full, and also so in conflict with each other, that he could really think of nothing else.

"Jesus sold Thomas into slavery?" Jan whispered to himself. He knew there was more in the book—he had read it in such haste that he knew in a second, and more careful reading, he would discover much more. But, more of what? Was the book a history of long-hidden truths, or was it a leather-bound cache of lies?

He was fascinated also with the eastern philosophy of it. Was Christianity, in the end, a mélange of the teachings of Buddha and the stories and laws of Judaism? He did not know enough about the former, since he had only heard talk of these monks from the east. There seemed to be much to admire…their self-discipline, their faith that all that happens is as it should be, their constant openness to new ideas, and this principle of wanting less. It was certainly difficult to dispute, Jan thought, that suffering comes from wanting what one does not have, and especially wanting what one knows they cannot ever get. Instead of promoting peace with one's Earthly life as the Buddhists do, we have been telling people to suffer through and their reward will come in the afterlife, that if they follow what the Church tells them, they will get into Paradise.

Jan clutched his head when he realized, and wondered, that if Christianity could be the result of a mixing of two older religions, might those two older religions be inspired by, be the inheritors of, the ideas of yet older religions? He decided to stop. Jan made the decision to not let his thoughts swirl this way. Humbly, he knew he did not possess the wisdom, nor did he have the mentorship of someone like Som, to guide himself through these thoughts. He would plant his feet and stand in service to God, and his son

Jesus, and to all the Saints, and to the Mystery, until he might grow wise and strong enough to entertain these thoughts again someday, if ever.

Jan coughed. He thought he should go fetch himself a drink, and perhaps eat something. He wished Pavel could have lived to read the book with him, and he wished he could discuss it with old Som Zec.

26

EMAUSKLOSTER
1944

RENATE ASKED, "BEFORE learning it in this book, have you ever in your life heard that St. Thomas had a son?"

Roman said, "I'd perhaps heard something about it."

"You knew, didn't you? You knew what was in the book? What I don't understand is what would Meinrer do with it? Germany is not at war with the Holy Church," Renate asked.

"It is always about convincing people that you have the 'real' truth. The Nazis are experts at this. If you can prove someone else has lied, or withheld the truth, even once, you gain an advantage in the war for people's trust. If Meinrer and his ilk can undermine the trust people have had in the Christian story for almost 2,000 years, many of them will become more susceptible to the narrative the Nazis want to spread. It is a war to control the narrative. Always," Roman said.

Renate said, "I knew many kind and compassionate people who became the most fervent Nazis. Once they had accepted what they were being told, once they had been made to fear immigrants, they were unwilling to even hear opposing viewpoints. They were taught, again and again, that anyone who disagreed with them, actually considered them stupid, so that even proposing a different viewpoint would cause them to become very angry, and reply with, 'I am not stupid, you know!' even though you had never suggested anything about their intelligence."

Roman said, "And then they were taught to feel superior to others, and this was like a drug, because so many had had feelings, often secret feelings, of inferiority, or that society was designed to keep them down, that their lives were a disappointment only because of the secret conspiracy of others, especially of those others who were different. The only way to get them to abandon this belief would be to get them to accept that their true station in life was what most of them had actually attained. That any shortcomings in their lives were likely due to choices they had made, or a lack of ability, a lack of effort, or simple bad luck. It is incredibly difficult to make people release a feeling of superiority in favor of accepting their own mediocrity. This has been done to people before, and it will happen again."

They sat quietly, in the dark, and then Roman felt her hand on his chest. He felt her breath on his face. He took her unseen face in his hands, and kissed her. She kissed back, passionately. Roman wrapped his arms around her, kissing her still, and felt her hands in his hair. Her hands moved to his face, and to his neck…and at this, he pulled away.

"What is wrong?" she whispered.

Before he could answer, air raid sirens began to wail once more.

"We should get the book, and you, away from this place," Roman said.

"You could come as well. We could try to get to Switzcrland, or somewhere else, wherever you want," she said.

Roman knew he was not going to Switzerland, but Meinrer must not get the book, and he and his men were likely still searching the monastery for them. Roman stood, tucked the book inside his robes, and took her hand. "If we are spotted, we must run for the exit, alright?" he asked.

"I will run with you," she said.

Still holding hands, they slid out through the narrow space, and back into the hallway. They began making their way out of the monastery.

27

EMAUZY
2022

CHRISTOPHE HAD OPENED his laptop, was typing furiously, and then said, “I don’t believe it. There is a grave in northern India. Yuz-Asaf, or St. Issa, known as Jesus of Nazareth to most people, is in a grave, inside a shrine in Srinagar, in Kashmir. Northern India.”

“Go on,” she said, as she stood and stretched.

“The shrine is known as Roz-Abal, on a street corner within the city. It’s not a secret, it’s on India’s tourist websites, even in a Lonely Planet travel guide. The locals believe that Jesus of Nazareth is buried there, beside a Muslim holy man who was added centuries later,” Christophe said.

“It’s in plain sight. The story has been out. People choose not to see it?” she asked.

“The narrative,” Christophe said.

"I think I heard something about this once, long ago, come to think of it. Maybe a British documentary," Professor Rossignol said.

"But you dismissed it, and even forgot about it," Christophe said. "It didn't fit with what you had already accepted as true."

"I suppose that's right. We can't go radically changing what we believe every day. We'd be lost," Professor Rossignol said.

"So, the question is, do we risk radically changing what billions believe, and disclose what is in this book?" Christophe asked. "I always wanted answers, when I was a boy, in church."

"You did?" she asked.

"I was even an altar boy, but I would ask the priest questions, and he would answer, which would only produce more questions. In fairness, the material he had to work with did contain a lot of contradictions, or changes anyway," Christophe said.

"What would a young boy ask? How difficult could it be for an educated man to answer?" she asked.

"I would ask the obvious ones, you know, like why would it be necessary to mark Cain after being banished, so that others would know him, when the sum total of the world's remaining population were his parents," he said.

"Ah yes," she said.

"But there were other things, like why does God

have to ask Adam to reveal himself in Eden? And the text reads that God 'walked' in the garden, looking for him. As opposed to later when he's a burning bush, or a disembodied voice. I would ask about these things," he said.

"Did the priest get angry?" she asked.

"He was a nice man, and patient. But what frustrated me most was when I pressed again and again, and he would eventually answer with, 'The Lord works in mysterious ways,' or 'It is not for us to know the mind of the Lord.' Those answers, even to me as a young boy, just seemed like he was ducking the questions," Christophe said.

"He was. Just as he'd been taught," she said.

A silence fell that was broken by a loud knock on the door, and Antonin coming into the office.

"They released you?" Christophe asked.

"They said they would make further inquiries, and I'm not to leave Prague," he said, and seemed to smile sadly at this.

"We have learned much," Professor Rossignol said, and she held up the book.

Antonin sat, as did the professor.

"Did you know that Jesus has a grave in Kashmir?" Christophe asked.

"In Srinagar," Antonin said.

"Of course you knew," Christophe said, shaking his head.

"The threatening notes you received were written by a Professor Sabatini," Antonin said. "They brought him in yesterday, and I heard him admit this. Apparently, he had been involved in some sort of disturbance at the Klementinum."

"He was. We were," Christophe said.

"When you got the book. You didn't tell me this," Professor Rossignol said.

Christophe shrugged, "We've been busy."

Antonin rose, walked to a window and quietly looked out.

"You knew where the book was, you knew what was in the book. Why involve us at all? If you wanted it hidden, it was. If you wanted it released to the world, you could have done this yourself," Christophe said.

Antonin turned and said, "I am weary. I am weary of the book, of its message, of worrying who might find it, of concern for what it might do to the world. Nearly my entire life has been centered around this book, and it has cost me a great deal. You have copies, and I will take the original."

"We have to keep the original, for continued study, to determine its origin, to establish its authenticity," Professor Rossignol said.

"You may keep a sample from its pages. As to its origin and history, I can help you with this. I know it very well," Antonin said.

28

MONASTERY OF THE SLAVS 1373

JAN WAS DREAMING and, in the dream, he was being washed away by a deep and fast-moving river current. On the bank, he saw his brother Petr running, calling out to him.

"Keep swimming, Jan! Swim!" Petr yelled.

Jan was trying to make for the bank, but with little progress. He lost sight of Petr, and yelled for him, choking, "Petr! Help me!"

It was then he spotted him, downstream, crawling out over the rushing water on a tree limb. As Petr came further and further out, the branch dipped lower and lower. Jan watched as his older brother slipped, and almost ended up in the river with him.

"Jan! Grab the branch! Grab it, Jan!" Petr called.

Attempting to swim and, at the same time, grabbing a branch seemed impossible. It wasn't a single bough, but instead Jan collided with a great mass of small branches. He clutched a handful, and came away with only twigs and leaves. Trying again, his left hand wrapped around something substantial just as he came through the other side of the branches. His feet immediately came to the surface. He grabbed with his right hand, and found purchase, but as he tried to pull himself to the branch, he found he wasn't strong enough.

"Petr, help me!" Jan said.

Petr tried to come farther out on the branch, but they both heard it cracking, and he retreated.

"Petr!" Jan said.

"I won't leave you, Jan, but I can't come to you!" he said.

"I'm not strong enough!" Jan said, and gulped a huge wave just then.

"Jan, you have to hold on! Do not let go! You are already saved, do NOT let go!" Petr said.

"How long must I hold on?" Jan asked.

"Until it releases you! Just fight and hold on!" Petr said.

"Do not leave me!" Jan said.

"I will stay right here!" Petr said. "You stay with me!"

Jan suddenly woke from his dream, and knew the pestilencia had him. He was shivering uncontrollably, drenched in sweat, and had not the strength to get out of his bed before relieving himself. He gripped the book tightly to his chest.

"Dearest Lord, forgive me if this book is a book of lies. If it is the truth, praise to you, Lord, that you allowed this humble servant to learn of it. My faith is not diminished, and my love for your Son, Jesus Christ, is only enlarged. Holy Mary, pray for me. My soul is prepared," Jan said, and then slipped back into fitful sleep once more.

29

EMAUSKLOSTER 1944

THE AIR RAID sirens continued, but this time it was different. Roman and Renate, in the hallway and trying to leave the monastery, could hear explosions in the city.

"There are bombs falling! It's an actual raid!" Renate said.

"Let's go back to the hiding spot! There are no windows and it will be one of the safest places in the monastery," Roman said. As they turned the corner, nearly back to the dark space, Meinrer and one of his soldiers were there and spotted them.

"Halt!" Meinrer shouted.

"Run!" Renate said. They sprinted back down the way they had come, and ran into the church. Roman led her toward the doors for the little side chapel, but before they got there, Meinrer's sergeant came through with his weapon leveled.

Meinrer entered the way they had, and asked, "Where is the book?"

The explosions outside grew louder, and the sergeant looked up and around. Meinrer came within a few steps of them, grabbed Renate by the arm, and pulled her away from Roman. Stepping backwards, his pistol aimed at Renate's abdomen, he said, "Enough of this, give me the damn book, or I will shoot her!"

Roman stepped to his left, next to the enormous bank of candles, and lifted the book above them.

"Burn it! Don't give it to him!" Renate said.

"You will shoot her and me the moment you have the book," Roman said.

"Possibly, but I will certainly shoot you and her if you burn that manuscript, so it seems we're at an impasse," Meinrer said.

"So, what do we do now?" Roman asked.

"Well, you see, it's all about cards to play," Meinrer said.

The explosions were close now, and the floor shook beneath them. The sergeant lowered his weapon as he looked toward the flashes visible now and then through the dark windows. There were fires burning in the streets of Prague.

"You have one card to play. To burn that book, or not. I have two cards to play. I can shoot her, and then

I can shoot you. You have five seconds until I play my first card," Meinrer said.

"If you shoot her, I will burn it," Roman said.

"And she will be dead, and I promise you that for weeks you will wish *you* were dead," Meinrer said. "Four seconds."

"Renate," Roman said.

"Don't give it to him!" she said.

"Two seconds," Meinrer said.

Just then, there was an explosion above, and the roof of the church collapsed. The force of the explosion, and the mass of air moved by the falling stone roof, threw Roman past the candles and into the doorway. His ears were ringing so badly, he could not hear anything except his own heartbeat. Pulling himself to one elbow, he saw nothing in the dark and dust. He knew the church was open to the night sky, but couldn't tell where dust ended and clouds began. Pulling himself up, he felt the book under his hand, and grasped it. Just as he got to his feet, another explosion drove him once more to the floor. There was a fire now in the church, and against the flames, he could see the silhouette of a mountain of debris and stone where Meinrer and Renate had stood.

"Renate!" he shouted. He put the book in his robes, went to where Renate had been, and he moved the smallest stone above where he thought she must be. He could barely lift it. He tried the next one, and was only able to cause it to roll off and fall beside the pile. The next, he could not even budge. Falling to his knees, he placed his hands on the pile, and sobbed. As his hearing slowly cleared, he could hear as the explosions became more distant. The flames inside the church, however, were drawing closer, and he could feel the heat on his skin. He subconsciously rubbed the old burn scar on his neck. Rising to his feet, he stumbled out through a ruined wall, very near where the windowsill had been that had, for so long, hidden the book. Looking out at the city, he could see the trail of devastation the bombers had left. Hundreds, at least, would be killed. Just as Renate was.

30

EMAUZY
2022

ANTONIN SAID, "YOU can have the ideas, the message, but you cannot have thc book itself."

"But you are only one source on the history of this book. We might learn a great deal scanning it, performing chemical tests on the pages and the ink," Christophe said.

"I can help with all of this, but then the book must be hidden, and I will go far from this place. It is time," Antonin said.

"What makes you so confident of your knowledge of this book?" Professor Rossignol asked.

"Because," Antonin said, "I have been either translating, protecting, or searching for this book since the first day it came here, to the Monastery of the Slavs, in 1373."

Christophe sat, mouth open, as Antonin rubbed

his neck, where there appeared to be a scar. "You're crazy," he said.

"You are very old," she mocked.

"Actually, no. By my calculation, I age about one month for every seven years that go by, although, that is only an estimate. About the book, I am not wrong, and you cannot keep it," Antonin said.

"It's not possible," she said.

"Is the book keeping you young?" Christophe asked.

"I suspect it has protected me from a great many things. I don't know why me, and not others. Perhaps because I was holding it when I died from the plague, and it brought me back. I have always been in proximity to it, even when I wasn't sure where it was hidden. For the past few decades, it has been in the Klementinum, where I have gone virtually every day. Moving it from place to place inside the building, I have kept it there since the war," he said.

"Because Emauzy was bombed, you couldn't leave it here," Christophe said.

"You are not believing this?" the professor asked.

In fact, Christophe could feel the truth of it. He couldn't explain it, but he knew that what Antonin was saying was true.

"The night the Americans mistakenly bombed Prague, and the monastery, the book left these walls, and did not return until you brought it back," Antonin said, looking at Christophe.

"Can't you tell at least one of us where you will take the book? Just in case?" Christophe asked.

"The temptation would be too great. I am sorry. You have your copies. I will allow you to have a cut corner of a page, with ink, for examination. Then, I will hide it again. I will say that, while I will not, the book will remain in Prague," Antonin said.

"This can't be? Can it?" she asked.

"Ask me anything, test me," Antonin said.

"But this would only prove that you are an expert on the history of this place," she said.

"Then perhaps we will have to take it on faith," Christophe said. "It costs us nothing to believe him. We can simply let go and choose to believe."

Antonin smiled a bit at this, and said, "In the end, it does not matter what you believe, but you are the first two in this century that I have told. Every time a secret is revealed, a bit more freedom, or perhaps a bit more light, has been created."

31

MONASTERY OF THE SLAVS 1373

JAN WOKE STILL clutching the book. His fever had broken. He sat up, weak and dizzy, but improved.

"How can this be?" he asked himself. He had seen people recover, but very few, and never from as sick as he had been. The light…he remembered a bright warm light, and the presence of old Som Zec, and peace. Had he died? Why would he be sent back, he of little consequence, when so many important people had died young and not returned?

It was the Lord, he thought, and his prayers. The book fell forward from his chest to lying flat on his lap. "The book. Is it the book?" he asked, but then he had a terrible realization. Had he not pulled it from poor Pavel's hands, would it have saved him? But, wait, no, he thought, Pavel in his state was going to burn it.

He then realized he was one of them. One of those

few who had recovered. Had they all experienced the light? Jan committed himself, anew, to a life of service.

He heard other monks outside. None had come to him, and none had cared for him. Sitting in his soiled bed, he wondered if they would have at least come and buried him. He decided he would not share this book and its message with them. Carefully returning to the refectory, he pulled the stone from beneath the window where Som Zec had hidden the book, and put it back. He replaced the stone, and promised himself he would return for the book someday.

He went back to his cell and cleaned, washing and replacing his bedding, cleansing the floor, table, and even refreshing the air as best he could. He then went to the baths, and cleansed himself, and it was here that Jan saw and spoke to other monks for the first time since reading the book. They were different somehow, and so was he. They were oldest of the brothers, some of them had been the most respected in the monastery, but he knew what they did not know. He blushed at the pride of it, and tried to suppress the feeling, but the vows—even the vow of chastity—now seemed artificial. According to the book, that was not an imitation of Jesus. It seemed it was a contrivance of some man, through the centuries, perhaps of someone unable to consummate the act himself, or perhaps it was the decree of a wise leader who recognized the power that priests would have over their flocks, and so took this potential indulgence away from them.

He could hear his elders discussing scripture around him that Jan wondered might be incorrect. When he heard the words, "…so he died that we might be saved," Jan thought, perhaps he did not die, but he was certainly grievously tortured for trying to bring peace to the hearts of his followers.

Jan never did pull the book from beneath that window again; history and its events prevented it.

32

KLEMENTINUM
1945

ROMAN WALKED SLOWLY in the Klementinum, through the enormous room with impossibly high ceilings, and a massive stove on one end. A stove that was more than three times as tall as Roman. There were rows of bookshelves here, and he searched for a few especially boring and inconsequential titles. Finding one on dairy cow husbandry next to an equally boring volume, Roman slid the book—the book given to Som Zec, the book Pavel had been so desperately sure could save him, the book a young Hussite named Vaclav found and hid again having never revealed it, the book that the Nazis wanted, the book he spent the last of his time with Renate discussing—in between those two dull books.

He stared at it for a moment, then dropped his head, made the sign of the cross, and headed back to Emauskloster. It had suffered terrible damage. Much of the church roof collapsed, one steeple was destroyed the night of the bombing, and the other burned down in the following days. For six days, the fires raged in the monastery. The heat caused deep cracks in the walls and an enormous amount of dust. The monastery's paintings were darkened with soot, and all the gilding had either melted or vaporized.

Now that the Nazis were gone from Prague, and defeated in their homeland, there was already talk of repairs and rebuilding the monastery, but with the new occupiers—the Soviets—and the system of government they brought with them, it seemed unlikely Emauskloster would go on being a center of faith and worship.

However, Roman knew that decades and centuries would pass by, and that in time, these Communists would eventually be gone as well, and perhaps, the monastery could be what it had once been.

33

EMAUZY
2022

PROFESSOR ROSSIGNOL AND Christophe made three more copies of the book, while Antonin sat and watched, and they placed them in three separate three-ring binders. Christophe did not bother making a coversheet, but on the edge of each binder, with a marker, he wrote, "The Twin."

"An interesting, if unrevealing, title," Antonin said. He stood, took a pair of scissors from the desk, opened the original manuscript to a page where he thought it would do the least damage, and cut a triangle from the page's corner. This he slipped inside the front cover of the top binder.

"It's agreed then. You'll stay the week with us as we work on a better translation, into French," Professor Rossignol said.

"And you promise to not immediately reveal what

you have found," Antonin said.

"To give you time to hide the book, and then get where you are going," said Christophe.

Antonin smiled, and said, "Yes, please wait, but you should not wait too long. There are other copies of… *The Twin*… in existence. Keep in mind that even the leather-bound copy I have is the translation of a much older document, from the first century. I have heard of other translations. I would much prefer that an honest translation from the two of you is released to the world before the words and story of Jesus can be twisted any more than they have been for the past 2,000 years."

"Where will you go?" Christophe asked, not sure if he would get an answer.

"I will go to Hemis, in Ladakh," he said.

"India," Professor Rossignol said, nodding.

"What will you look for there?" Christophe asked, "Are you trying to find the origin of the book? Or the older version?"

"I am not seeking answers, and I am not even looking for more questions. No evidence, no proof. No more secrets," Antonin said.

"What then?" Christophe asked.

Antonin looked up at the ceiling, and then at Christophe, and said, "An end."

"But Antonin, think of the history you could share," she said.

He said, "My name is Jan, actually, *finally*. And if I did as you suggest, I would simply be adding one more narrative."

NOTICE

THE TWIN—WHICH IS represented in this story as an ancient book that was translated into Glagolitic—actually exists. It is another novel, published by Encircle Publications, written by Kevin St. Jarre, and available in hardcover, paperback, and e-book wherever good books are sold.

At the end of this edition of *The Book of Emmaus*, Encircle has included the first chapter of *The Twin*, with our best wishes.

ACKNOWLEDGMENTS

THE FIRST WORDS of this manuscript were written in Prague at a table downstairs at the Maitrea restaurant, very near the Old City Square, on Tynská ulička. The food was delicious.

After spending time in the Emauzy monastery, the first third of the novel was written in an apartment on Šmeralova street, in Prague 7, between Letná Park and Stromovka Park.

Some was also written in the amazing Klementinum, in the General Study Room or *Studovna*, a beautiful workspace that was well worth spending the US$0.45 for a ticket. It's centuries old and has WiFi that, unlike at a nearby coffeeshop at Malostranské námestí, actually worked.

I finished the first draft of this novel while staying at Hewnoaks Artist Colony in Lovell, Maine, in a small cottage called "Sans Souci," sitting at a well-worn plywood desk, looking out floor-to-ceiling corner windows at Kezar Lake. It was an inspiring place to work. Visual artists, writers, fabric artists, sculptors, musicians, filmmakers, actors… all sorts of creatives are welcome to apply, and each person gets their own space, in their own cottage. Find Hewnoaks on social media, and online at www.hewnoaks.org for more information on how to apply for a residency.

As always, huge thanks to the entire team at Encircle Publications. Your support, hard work, talent, friendship, and faith are always deeply appreciated. This is my fifth novel that you have so graciously shepherded out into readerland. The entire process has always been so much fun. From the initial explanations of what the book is, to the editorial responses from your team, to the first glimpses of a new cover… and then that day that the first printed author's copies arrive, and then the launch date when the story suddenly catapults across the country and around the world into the hands of readers, it's always a wonderful adventure with you all. Thank you to Eddie, Cynthia, Deirdre, Chris, Michael, and everyone at Encircle.

This novel represents the very first thing I began writing while my mother, Cecile (Thibodeau) St. Jarre was still alive, and that I completed after we lost her to cancer in November 2020. Long before I got anywhere near a school, she taught me to read, and to love books. She cheered on any creative work I produced, whether it was writing or visual art.

Mom once said if she could've been anything, she would've liked to have been an archeologist, sifting through history's mysteries. I hope she would've liked this book.

Thank you to my son, Dmitri, who let me walk through the entire outline for this novel, bouncing ideas off of him and listening to his feedback, while he was feeling pretty under the weather during a medical battle he was fighting. He provided ideas and support at other times, too. I'm looking forward to hearing what he thinks of the final product.

Some dates and history were adapted to tell this story. To learn more about the real Emauzy, the Benedictine Abbey Na Slovenech, in Prague, go online at https://opatstvi-emauzy.cz or go to Prague and see it for yourself. If you do go, regardless of your beliefs, be thoughtful, and speak softly, in a place of such history, faith, and ghosts.

ABOUT THE AUTHOR

KEVIN ST. JARRE is also the author of *Aliens, Drywall, and a Unicycle*, *Celestine*, and *The Twin*, and *Absence of Grace*, each published by Encircle Publications. He previously penned three original thriller novels for Berkley Books, the Night Stalkers series, under a pseudonym. He's a published poet, his pedagogical essays have run in *English Journal* and thrice in *Phi Delta Kappan*, and his short fiction has appeared in journals such as *Story*.

Kevin has worked as a teacher and professor, a newspaper reporter, an international corporate consultant, and he led a combat intelligence team in the first Gulf War. Kevin is a polyglot, and he earned an MFA in Creative Writing with a concentration in Popular Fiction from University of Southern Maine's Stonecoast program. Twice awarded scholarships, he studied at the Norman Mailer Writers Center on Cape Cod, Massachusetts, with Sigrid Nunez and David Black, and wrote in southern France at La Muse Artists & Writers Retreat.

He is a member of MWPA and the International Thriller Writers. Born in Pittsfield, Massachusetts, Kevin grew up in Maine's northernmost town, Madawaska. He now lives on the Maine coast, and is always working on the next novel. Follow Kevin at www.facebook.com/kstjarre and on Twitter @kstjarre.

If you enjoyed reading this book,
please consider writing your honest review
and sharing it with other readers.

Many of our Authors are happy to participate in Book Club and Reader Group discussions. For more information, contact us at info@ encirclepub.com.

Thank you,
Encircle Publications

For news about more exciting new fiction, join us at:

Facebook: www.facebook.com/encirclepub

Instagram: www.instagram.com/encirclepublications

Twitter: twitter.com/encirclepub

Sign up for Encircle Publications newsletter and specials: eepurl.com/cs8taP

Excerpt from *The Twin*

AMONG HIS CLOSEST followers there were three of us named Judas. There was the Iscariot. There was also Judas, the younger brother of James, whom we called Taddai as a term of endearment. As for me, I am known as Judas the Twin, or in Aramaic—Tau'ma. I am called Thomas, and perhaps known best for doubt born of grief.

It was winter, my thirteenth year, when they came. Their robes were dyed with pigments such as saffron, creating layers of color on each man ranging from pale gold to a deep red. There were eight monks in all, but there were many more who had traveled with them.

They came to the palace of Herod a year before the king's death. It was in Jerusalem that they met with Herod, and not Jericho as some have claimed. I know because I was there. I worked there as a craftsman, one of many. I saw them entering and I followed. By the time they reached the court, I was more within their group than without.

Appearing before Herod, king of the Jews and son of Antipater, and his ministers, the [indecipherable] of them, spoke for the group. He spoke in Greek. "I am called Dawa. We have traveled from the east. There was a sign of a birth, a sign in the sky, in the spring before last."

His words were a bit clumsy, but his Greek was nearly as good as my own. Herod said nothing. The ministers, courtiers, the crowd altogether, was silent.

"There was a bright light, stars came together. We believe such signs show us the way," Dawa said.

The crowd began to whisper the word, "Magi. Magi." They took these men to be followers of a religion much focused on astrology, however Dawa and his companions were not Magi, nor were they even Persian.

Dawa said, "We seek our spiritual leader, a great holy man. He left us two years ago. We began watching for some sign of where the holy child might be born. The sign appeared and bade us travel west, to your land, before it faded and was gone. It was bright and one among them was red. Do you remember it?"

The stars. I remembered them well, as did we all. A bright rope of stars. However, it had not appeared to our west. The crowd buzzed now, excited. No one spoke directly to Dawa until Herod nodded slightly to one of his ministers, a man named Ptolemaeos. He turned to Dawa and said, "The stars were to our south. They were close. It seemed one could have walked directly beneath them in half a night."

Dawa turned to his companions and whispered something. He then turned back and asked, "Is there a village or town nearby to the south?"

Herod himself suddenly said, "You seek a king." His face was dark, his tone menacing. A chill passed through me. I doubted Dawa understood with whom he was dealing. Herod had killed his own sons and wife out of fear for his throne.

Dawa seemed momentarily confused. "Our guide. We come to find him."

Herod asked, "And his child will be born here?"

Dawa was patient. "Not his child." He paused for a moment, apparently searching his Greek. "The spirit of our holy one would have returned to be born of man on Earth with [indecipherable] in time."

"Why would your holy spirit make pregnant a woman in Judea?" Herod asked.

Dawa frowned and looked back to his fellow travelers. He turned back and said, "Great king. We believe our guide has returned to show us the way."

Herod rose. "There is a village to the south. Bethlehem. Go there and find him. When you discover the child, send me word so that I, too, may adore your newly born leader."

Dawa asked, "Might one of your men come with us, to show us the way to this village?"

Herod's face became grim. I knew that he did not want to send any of his men, because this would have caused fear among those the travelers might question. Herod scanned the room until his eyes fell on me.

"Take him with you," Herod said, pointing. All in the room turned to me. I looked from Herod to Dawa. The latter smiled and nodded slightly. I felt a sudden calm settle upon me. I would take them to Bethlehem.

I walked along with them. Bethlehem was not difficult to find. I did not object to going but I was not sure why they had asked for a guide. One simply needed to walk south on that one road until sunset and he would arrive in Bethlehem. Of course, this group of men, camels, and horses would take longer. They stopped often. None of the men rode the animals, instead walking alongside. The animals carried burdens and pulled carts.

Dawa approached me as we walked. "What do you do for the king?"

"I am a craftsman," I answered.

"In wood?" he asked.

I said, "Mostly stone, there is little wood in this part of Judea. The craftsmen here, homebuilders and tool makers, work with metals and stone."

He did not immediately respond. I was not sure he had understood my Greek until he asked, "How long have you worked in your trade?"

"I began apprenticing at the end of my seventh year," I said.

Dawa was quiet again.

"Are you an astrologer?" I asked. "By trade?"

He said, "I am a student."

"Are you a slow learner?" I asked. He had no hair and no whiskers but the lines in his face betrayed him to be a man of at least forty years.

Dawa laughed. It was a rich sound, unencumbered. The laughter of a child. I hadn't laughed like that since before my apprenticeship began and I would not laugh that way for some years to come.

He said, "I am a slow learner. I believe many of us are slow." His grin was broad. "What do they call you?"

I was not smiling, nor was I offended at his laughing at my question. I was curious. I said, "I am called Judas, the twin. You may call me that. You may call me Thomas."

"Why are you called the twin? Have you a brother?" Dawa asked.

The caravan stopped suddenly. We both looked ahead. There was no obstruction, nothing to impede our progress.

"Why have we stopped again?" I asked.

Dawa answered without looking at me. "Why not stop?"

"Because it will take us well into the night to get to Bethlehem at this rate," I said. "Will we wake the village looking for your king?"

Dawa turned to face me. "Not a king. A guide. Our friend."

"But the child was recently born, how can you know him?" I asked.

Dawa sat on the edge of the road and invited me join him. I looked ahead, saw men casually talking. I sighed and sat.

"We believe that when someone's body dies, his spirit lives on and is reborn into a new life," Dawa said. "Our friend was a very holy man, very special. Soon after he died, we began watching for signs as to where he might next arrive. The signs led us here."

"You believe that the spirit of your dead friend will be inside the child you seek? Like a possession?" I asked.

"Not as two struggling for control of one body. The body will be rightly and solely his," Dawa said.

I paused and then asked, "How will you know the child when you find him?"

"We will give the child an ancient test," Dawa said. His voice sounded calm and sure.

"What will you do with the child?" I asked.

Dawa said, "If we find our friend, we will explain the situation to his mother and father."

"Isn't your friend's spirit the father? You told Herod that the spirit made the woman pregnant," I said.

"I did not say that," Dawa said. "I said only that we believe our guide has returned."

Many of the men were sitting by this time. I wanted to find the child. I said, "I should go ahead and find the child before you arrive. Then I will lead you to him and you can test him."

"Thomas," Dawa said, "let me tell you a story. A man told his son one night, 'Tomorrow we will go to the village and bring something back.' The next morning the son woke very early and without asking any more from his father, set out for the village on his own. When he reached the village, he was already very tired. He also realized that he did not know what his father had intended to bring back from the village. He returned to his father, so hungry and thirsty and exhausted he believed he might die. His father thought him a fool for suffering so much without purpose or accomplishment."

I understood immediately and my face grew hot. I asked, "Why not simply tell me to stay quiet and not go to the village rather than tell me this story to embarrass me?"

Dawa smiled. "Stories reveal their lessons to those who are ready to learn. They also carry their lessons across languages and lifetimes. Whenever you teach, Thomas, try to teach with stories." Dawa stood and walked toward the lead elements of the caravan. The other men rose slowly in response and the caravan began to move again.

Being their guide, I thought I should follow.

www.ingramcontent.com/pod-product-compliance
Lightning Source LLC
Chambersburg PA
CBHW020330030826
48979CB00021B/512